'So you didn' **thoughts about**

Determined not to little else, Serina shook her head emphatically. 'Certainly not.'

'That sure is a pity,' he murmured as he plundered her lips again.

She pushed him away gently and smiled archly. 'You know my reasons for coming out to Alberta—they don't include a casual affair.'

'Oh, Serina, I wish as much as you that things could be different, but they can't. . .ever!'

Born in the industrial north, **Sheila Danton** trained as a Registered General Nurse in London, before joining the Air Force nursing service. Her career was interrupted by marriage, three children and a move to the West Country where she now lives. She soon returned to her chosen career, training and specialising in Occupational Health, with an interest in preventative medicine. Sheila has now taken early retirement, and is thrilled to be able to write full time.

Recent titles by the same author:

A PRIVATE AFFAIR

DOCTOR'S DILEMMA

BY
SHEILA DANTON

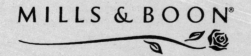

MILLS & BOON®

All the characters in this book have no existence outside the imagination of the author, and have no relation whatsoever to anyone bearing the same name or names. They are not even distantly inspired by any individual known or unknown to the author, and all the incidents are pure invention.

*First published in Great Britain 1997
Harlequin Mills & Boon Limited,
Eton House, 18-24 Paradise Road, Richmond, Surrey TW9 1SR*

© Sheila Danton 1997

ISBN 0 263 80210 8

*Set in Times 10 on 10 pt. by
Rowland Phototypesetting Limited
Bury St Edmunds, Suffolk*

03-9708-54815-D

*Printed and bound in Great Britain
by Mackays of Chatham PLC, Chatham*

CHAPTER ONE

THE excitement that had been simmering during Serina Grant's first trip across the Atlantic boiled over as she emerged from the arrivals hall at Alberta City Airport. She knew that she was probably expecting far too much from the trip as she tried to identify her mother's old friend in the waiting crowd, but she didn't care.

For the first time in her life she was free to do whatever she pleased. A momentary sadness swept through her at the memory of her recent loss, but she refused to allow it to swamp her excitement.

What was it that her late mother's friend, Coral, had said in her last letter? 'I'll be with my daughter, Heather. We're both of average height, but she's as thin as I'm fat!'

The only couple obviously answering the description were at the front of the small group, the elder of the pair gazing into a camcorder eyepiece.

Only a handful of passengers had remained for the last stage of the flight from Calgary, so Serina looked round curiously to see whom they were filming. The only person emerging behind her was a sun-tanned hunk of a man, carrying a bulging briefcase. His dark wavy hair was immaculately styled, every hair precisely in place. He was striding confidently towards the camera, an air of unquestionable authority oozing from every pore.

Wondering if she should recognise him as someone famous, Serina saw the younger girl wave and turned to see if it was returned. It wasn't immediately, but after a few seconds he gave an embarrassed lift of his hand.

Serina had more important things to do than observe their reunion, so she looked around eagerly for anyone else answering Coral's description.

With a sudden frown she watched the sparse crowd rapidly disperse with the few remaining passengers, and her happiness evaporated as she realised that there was no one to meet her.

A tap on her shoulder made her start nervously, and she turned to find herself looking up into eyes so dark that, until their owner turned slightly towards the light, she thought they were black.

'Heather wants you to walk towards her mother so she can film your arrival close up.' It was the reluctant film star speaking, his overt masculinity threatening to overwhelm her jaded senses.

Confused, she turned in the direction he indicated but saw only the original couple. Seeing the young girl beckon her, she walked hesitantly towards them. Abandoning the camcorder, the elder of the two—whom she presumed must be Coral—flung her arms round Serina. 'Welcome to Canada.'

Serina said uncertainly, 'Who—? I thought you were filming him.' She turned to point out the dark-suited man who'd tapped her shoulder, but he'd disappeared. 'The one who just spoke to me, I mean.'

Coral laughed. 'I was filming *you*. Greg is a doctor at the hospital where I work. He's been away in Calgary for a few days and must have cajoled his way onto your flight. He was puzzled by the camera as well. He wasn't expecting a reception committee!'

'Poor chap. I thought he looked embarrassed,' Serina laughed.

'I knew who you were instantly,' Coral confided, appraising her from head to toe. 'You're so like your mother, Serina. The same dark hair that doesn't usually come with eyes such a deep blue. And that smile. The likeness is incredible. You must miss her dreadfully.'

Coral's reminder that she was now alone in the world sobered Serina's mood for an instant, but she lifted her chin defiantly and said, 'It's not been easy, but there's no point in dwelling on the past. Mum would be the first to remind me that life has to go on.'

Coral nodded. 'She was that kind of person. Do anything for anyone. She was so good to me before I came to Canada that I'd hoped to repay her with a holiday. Especially when she was so ill. But it wasn't to be.' Her eyes clouded momentarily. 'Still, she'd be glad to know that I'm doing it for you instead.'

Determined not to allow the trauma of the recent months to dominate her life a moment longer, Serina smiled. 'She certainly valued your friendship and spoke of you often. I'm really looking forward to getting to know you all. And the farm.'

'Right,' Coral said briskly. 'This is all your luggage? You certainly travel light. Let's get it to the car.'

As they walked, Serina surreptitiously examined them both. Coral truly was as round as a barrel, but she radiated hospitality. A real earth mother, Serina guessed. Heather was totally the opposite. Appearing much younger than her twenty-two years, her petite slenderness endowed her with an elfin prettiness. At five feet eight Serina felt a giant by comparison, despite her trim shape.

Suddenly conscious of Heather's interested perusal of the comfort-cut jeans she'd worn for travelling, Serina intercepted her gaze and smiled.

'Was it a good flight?' the young girl asked hurriedly.

'Fine. I've never flown long distance before, and wasn't particularly looking forward to it, but it seemed that we'd hardly left England before we were approaching Calgary.'

As Coral helped Serina to load the luggage into a dust-covered car of indeterminate make and colour Heather drew their attention to the long-limbed man pacing furiously up and down in the evening sunshine.

'It's Greg—Dr Pardoe. On the other side of the car park. Do you think something is wrong?'

Coral slammed down the boot with a frown. 'I'll go and ask him.'

'Mum'll soon sort it out. Let's get in.' She moved towards the front of the car.

Serina opened the rear door, but as she was about to do as suggested Heather said, 'Would you rather sit in the front?'

It was obvious that Heather wasn't keen to relinquish her usual place, so Serina murmured, 'This is fine, thanks.'

She settled herself as Coral returned with the man who

had spoken to her earlier. 'Greg arranged for his car to be waiting for him, but it's not here. I've said we'll take him home.'

Heather began to climb out of the front seat, but he stopped her. 'I'll be OK in the back, thanks.' He slid his impressively muscular physique in beside Serina, his dark eyes alight with an appreciative smile that set her pulse racing.

Coral turned in her seat. 'Serina Grant, meet Greg Pardoe.'

They both nodded and Greg took her hand firmly in his. 'I gather we travelled together from Calgary.' With his thumb, he unconsciously caressed the hand he was holding with a light touch that sent the pleasantest of sensations scudding along to her nerve endings.

Raising her eyes, she saw that he was searching her face with eyes that smouldered with an indefinable emotion. 'Pity I didn't know you were arriving today. I could have made the last part of your trip more interesting by pointing out a few landmarks.'

It wasn't so much the words he said but the way he said them which evoked the emotional storm deep within her. Not ready for such a response, she sought to release the tension between them with a laugh. 'It was such a short flight that I don't think we'd have got past the introductory stage!'

He nodded his amused agreement and reluctantly allowed her to free her hand from his strong grasp before asking, 'You're related to Coral?'

'No, she and my mother trained together in England.'

Serina sensed a sudden puzzled withdrawal on Greg's part. In the confines of the car it seemed almost physical as he enquired, 'So she would have known my mother as well? She trained with Coral.'

Serina frowned. 'I don't think so. As far as I know, Coral was the only person she knew over here.'

'That's rather strange, surely? If she knew Coral, she must have known Mum.'

Serina was thrown by his accusatory tone. 'What are you trying to say?'

Coral, who had obviously been listening closely, broke in, 'Give her a break, Greg. Her mother died just a couple of months ago. I've asked her out here to get over it.'

'Sorry. I didn't realise. But they would have known one another, surely?' Despite his apologetic words, Serina saw that he was watching her with a definite query in his narrowed eyes.

'There were a lot of us, Greg,' Coral answered, before Serina could speak.

'Yes, but—'

'Cool it, Greg.'

He shrugged impatiently, but did change the direction of his questioning. 'What do the rest of your family think about you deserting them at this time?'

'There's no one.'

'Family, you mean? What about your father?'

Her blue eyes troubled, Serina didn't answer immediately.

'Won't he miss you?'

'I never knew him.'

Coral saved the day again. 'Greg! She's been through a lot recently.'

'OK.' His smile had disappeared, and Serina felt like a specimen under the microscopic inspection to which he was subjecting her.

Wondering what hidden conflicts she had accidentally stumbled across, she raised her hand and nervously smoothed her dark hair, before turning away to watch the scenery flashing by. He still wasn't put off, though. He dropped the cross-examination about her family, and asked instead, 'What do you do for a living?'

'I'm a nurse.'

'Are you hoping to work over here?'

'I don't think so.'

'You're just on holiday, then?'

Why did she get the feeling that he now disapproved of everything she said? 'At the moment. If I like it here and find suitable work I may come back again, but I have no definite plans.'

'Nursing?'

'I don't mind. If I decide I want to settle here I'm prepared to do anything.'

'You may have to—we've enough unemployed nurses of our own.'

Angry now, Serina retorted, 'In that case, I'll just enjoy my holiday. I guess nursing wouldn't be the same over here, anyway.'

'You think we're still in the dark ages, do you?'

'That wasn't what I meant,' she defended hotly, desperately trying to work out a reason for the change in his manner towards her.

'What's your speciality?'

'I—er—nothing in particular. Recently I've done agency work so that I could look after Mum.'

'I see.'

Once again she detected an almost imperceptible disapproval in his voice and was puzzled, especially after his initial welcome had suggested that he hadn't exactly found her unattractive. She couldn't recall having said anything to make him think she lacked commitment, but what other reason could there be?

Determined to prove otherwise, she said, 'Before Mum became ill I was working with the elderly. A rehab ward for both acute and chronically ill.'

'Did you enjoy it?'

She sensed her answer had actually stirred his interest, so started to elaborate. 'I got a real sense of satisfaction from it. Unlike some of the nursing homes I've worked in since.'

'I can imagine,' he responded, reverting to a critical tone.

Becoming increasingly annoyed, Serina shot him a black look before she turned to watch the city streets flashing by. He was certainly good-looking, but his manners left much to be desired.

She was saved from further interrogation by Coral asking, 'Have you eaten, Greg? We can stop and get a bite before we leave the city, or get something later.'

His dark eyes flashed a challenge at Serina as he answered, '*I* can wait. How about you?'

'That's fine by me.' As it happened, she wasn't particularly hungry, but even had she been starving she would not have admitted it. 'How far *is* home, Coral?'

Greg answered. 'About ninety kilometres.'

'I didn't realise it was so far.' Her composure already ruffled by his response to her, she tried to suppress the surprise in her voice.

They were emerging from wide city streets onto a fast road that bisected a vast expanse of unspoilt countryside. 'It's incredible—so much space.' Serina breathed the words almost without thinking.

Greg nodded. 'I couldn't agree more. The only time I went to England I felt like Gulliver must have done in Lilliput. I sure was glad to be back in the wide open spaces.'

Serina decided not to give him the satisfaction of rising to his insult to her home country. Instead, she pretended to be interested in the passing scenery, but she took in none of it. Her mind was too busy wondering just what Greg Pardoe's problem was. She'd come out to spend a holiday with her mother's friend and she didn't need his hang-ups about England or his mother.

There was little traffic so Coral was able to maintain a steady speed until the car eventually turned off onto a dusty road; then they progressed at little more than walking pace.

'Nearly there,' Greg informed her.

Coral appeared to be manoeuvring along ruts in the road that weren't exactly making the driving easy. The choking dust her wheels threw up explained the state of the car's exterior.

'Will you join us for a bite to eat, Greg, or do you want to go straight to Greenfield?'

'That sounds great—I've nothing to hurry back for, but I'd better ring and check what's happened to my car.'

'I can take you back later.' Heather turned her head to make the offer with a winsome smile.

Greg nodded his thanks as Coral swung into a smaller and even more pitted road that led down to an isolated bungalow. 'This is it. Home sweet home.'

Greg leapt from his side of the car and, opening

Heather's door for her, smiled warmly.

Was that why he'd been so tetchy in the car? Would he have preferred to sit by Heather? Serina was too tired to care. She'd dealt with enough problems of her own recently, without worrying about not living up to *his* expectations.

'I've put you in the basement, Serina. You have it all to yourself.' Coral led the way downstairs to a large cool area and through to a bedroom at the far end. 'The bathroom's next door, so help yourself. Ed is already in bed and asleep—with harvest approaching he has to be up early in the morning.'

Once alone, Serina looked around her at the typically English floral furnishings and felt immediately at home. She unpacked quickly and made her way up the stairs into the kitchen where Heather and Greg were in close conversation. The moment they saw her they stopped talking, giving Serina the uncomfortable feeling that they had been discussing her.

'Cup of tea?' Coral came into the room and broke the silence.

Serina nodded. 'Lovely.'

'We can eat soon. You must both be tired.'

Serina checked her watch and saw that it was approaching four in the morning, British time. 'You can say that again,' she murmured. 'I feel like I usually do on night duty.'

Throughout the snack meal Heather and Greg conversed about people she didn't know, and when she'd finished eating Serina felt her eyes closing.

'Don't worry about clearing away, Serina. Get off to bed.'

When she protested Coral told her, 'We have a dishwasher. Now be off with you.'

Bidding the three of them a goodnight, she thankfully did as she was told.

Despite her tiredness, she didn't sleep immediately. She couldn't help wondering about the reason for Greg's sudden hostility towards her. Surely it couldn't be because she denied all knowledge of his mother? Or was it because she was English and he hadn't enjoyed a stay in that country? Surely someone with enough intelligence to become a doctor would not react in that way for such a trivial reason?

She would try and find out more about him from Coral the next day. She didn't yet feel comfortable enough with the immature Heather to ask her.

She slept eventually but woke late the next morning. Coral was alone in the kitchen.

'Hi. Coffee?'

'Thanks.' Serina held out three gift-wrapped packages. 'This one's for you.'

As she took them Coral shook her head. 'We didn't expect you to do anything like this.'

'I wanted you to have something typically English. Be careful, it's breakable.'

Coral unwrapped a blue glass jug. 'It's beautiful,' she breathed as she scanned the accompanying leaflet. 'Made in the West Country, I see.' She kissed Serina's cheek. 'Thank you so much. I shall treasure it.' She placed the jug on the window-sill, where the morning sunlight enhanced its beauty. 'Now, would you like toast? Or cereal?'

'Just a slice of toast, please.'

'Did you sleep OK?'

'Fine. The bed is so comfortable I could have stayed there all day!'

'Glad to hear it. We can do a tour of the farm in what's left of this morning and then after lunch we'll pop into Greenfield and I'll show you where I work.'

'Which ward are you on?'

'We don't have wards as such. I work in long-term care.'

'Is that for the elderly?'

'In theory it's supposed to be for patients of any age needing extended care, but mostly it's used like a residential or nursing home in England. The residents can bring in their own bed if they want to, and although most rooms are single we do have the odd double if a husband and wife prefer it.'

When they moved outside Serina couldn't get over the

immense size of the fields and the machinery necessary to cope with such an acreage. 'It's so different from the English countryside, isn't it?' she said to Coral as they sat outside for a lunch of sandwiches.

'I guess so. I've got so used to the wide open spaces that I don't think about it. I suppose Heather would notice the difference if she visited England.'

'I can see that. Does she help out on the farm?' Serina was grateful for the opportunity to ask about Heather. And Greg's involvement in her life.

'She works in an office. She has to drive about fifty kilometres each way, but it's a good job and has prospects.'

'She didn't follow you into nursing, then? Like I did Mum?'

'No.'

'But she knows Greg?'

'The social life out here is very limited, as I'm sure you can imagine. Most events are centred on the town and often on the hospital, so all the youngsters know one another.'

She didn't elaborate, leaving Serina still unsure if there was anything more than friendship between the couple.

As they cleared away after lunch Serina tried another tack. 'Do you know Greg's mother?'

Coral nodded. 'As he said, we trained together and came out here around the same time so we've kept in touch.'

'So Mum *must* have known her.'

'We were a large group,' she replied evasively. 'I don't remember half of them now so I don't expect your mum did either.' Sure that Coral was not telling her the whole truth, Serina made up her mind to broach the subject again when she knew Coral better. However, she did ask, 'Did I unwittingly say something to upset Greg in the car yesterday?'

Coral shook her head. 'No—don't think that. Greg—er, well—er—put it like this, I've known him and his mother for a long time and, to put it bluntly, life hasn't been easy for either of them. He's had to work hard to get where he is and I suppose he saw you as a link to his mother's problems. That's all. Right, ready now to storm the big "city" of Greenfield?'

Although she wanted to ask how she could possibly be linked, Serina was aware that the subject was being tactfully changed and could do nothing but agree.

She was able to sit in the front of the car this time and so could appreciate just how vast and uninhabited was the prairie they were driving through. Coral edged out onto the dusty road and headed in the opposite direction to their arrival the night before.

As they entered a sparsely built-up area she pointed to a building on the other side of the wide boulevard. 'That's the old hospital. I worked there when I first arrived in Alberta. The Province gave us a new building a few years ago. Goodness know why. They can't afford to run it now.'

She pulled up in a spacious car park and Serina let out an involuntary gasp.

'I didn't expect it to be so large for such a small town.'

Coral laughed ruefully. 'Although Greenfield has a population of under a thousand, the unit has a largish catchment area. But I'm afraid it's not all in use—one wing is shut.'

'It's not called a hospital, then,' Serina queried as she noted the sign by the front entrance saying HEALTH CARE UNIT.

Coral laughed. 'I still call it "the hospital" but, yes, that's its correct title.' She led the way into a spacious and airy central entrance hall.

'Hi, Coral,' a smart receptionist greeted her. 'Can't keep away, even on your day off?'

'This is a nursing friend from England. I thought she'd like to see our set-up.'

'Pleased to meet you.' The attractive young girl gave her a friendly smile as Greg materialised behind the nursing station and slid an arm along her shoulder. He then gave her a friendly wink, before turning to Serina and asking in a far from cordial tone, 'Come to check up on us?'

As the receptionist was obviously surprised by his coolness Serina decided to ignore it, and gave him her brightest smile. 'It's always interesting to see how other hospitals function.'

'Oh, goodness, duty calls. Show her around for me, Greg.' Coral tossed the command over her shoulder as she sped into the dining area to help a patient struggling in vain to lift a spoon to her mouth.

'It'll be a privilege,' he murmured, before leading the way past several utility rooms to corridors which Serina saw contained the patients' rooms.

Aware that he didn't mean it, she followed slowly. 'Please don't worry about me. I'm sure you have more important things to attend to.'

'Perhaps, but they can wait. I'd like to show you just how well we *do* do things.'

Exasperated by his unjust perception of her, she snapped, 'That's the last thing—'

Her words were interrupted by him suddenly swinging round and into a sitting area. 'Are you OK, Max?'

The patient he spoke to was slumped over a table in the corner. When he didn't answer Greg checked his pulse and frowned.

'Grab a wheelchair and help me take him back to his room.'

Not expecting the order or having a clue where to find a wheelchair, Serina didn't move immediately. 'Where—?'

'If you'd rather not help, search out one of the nurses. Quickly.'

Serina raced back to the reception desk. 'Wheelchair?' she asked urgently.

The receptionist pointed to a room behind the desk. Serina found what she was looking for and, opening it up, wheeled it rapidly back to the sitting area.

'You found one!' Greg's features registered surprise, tempered with what Serina hoped was a grudging approval. 'Come on, old chap,' he murmured gently, 'let's get you back to bed.' Greg placed both hands beneath Max's arms and lifted him bodily. Serina pulled the chair away and replaced it with the wheelchair. Greg lowered the patient into it. 'Well done.'

She raised an eyebrow but said nothing although, searching his face, she thought she detected just a hint of the appreciation he'd exhibited the day before.

Grasping the handles of the wheelchair, he set off at a brisk pace and Serina followed. She saw that they were in the right room because on the wall outside was a hand-crafted wall plaque containing a photograph of the occupant, together with his full name.

'What a brilliant idea,' she murmured.

Greg turned and, seeing what she was looking at, agreed. 'For staff and patients alike. A wonderful memory prompt.'

When Serina was in the room with him he closed the door, before saying, 'Let's get him undressed and into bed.'

This time Max responded to Greg's voice and mumbled, 'Why?'

'You fell asleep, so we're getting you into bed for a rest. And aren't you the lucky one? We have a nurse from England helping.'

Max looked up at Serina with an approving glint in his eye.

Helping her to slide Max's shirt over his head, Greg bantered with a grin, 'Don't get too excited, Max. She's only here to look around. She just happened to be handy when I needed someone to help.'

'Pity. You should persuade her to stay.'

'She doesn't want to.'

He didn't want her to was more like it, she thought wryly.

Once Max was in bed Greg left her to go in search of someone to relieve them both. Serina made her patient comfortable, and when he closed his eyes again she folded his clothes tidily.

When Greg came back with a young girl in tow, he raised a surprised eyebrow at the order she'd created. 'Looks like it's all done, Kathy. But perhaps you'd stay and keep an eye on his obs for the time being.'

Serina felt a quiet satisfaction at having made another small dent in his inexplicable prejudice.

As they left the room she queried, 'Transient ischaemic attack?'

'I guess so—a small clot has probably cut off the blood

supply to part of his brain. He had something similar the
other day, but the nurse who found him on the floor said
that he had no residual symptoms so, although I couldn't
be absolutely sure, I ordered various investigations.

'Today, as you saw for yourself, when he first came
round he had a definite weakness on the left side, which
is already fading.'

Serina nodded. 'Do you give aspirin in these cases?'

He gave her a questioning glance. 'You don't expect
us to use modern treatments over here?'

'I don't understand why you take everything I say as a
criticism. I wasn't implying anything of the sort.'

He countered, 'But?'

'Not all doctors back home agree on its use, especially
the dosage,' she retorted defensively.

'Max is on 75 mg alternate days. We'll need to rethink
that, following this attack. Now we're sure what we're
dealing with I'll set up some more tests and try and discover the root of the trouble. We need to prevent him
progressing to a full-blown stroke or even a heart attack.
Now, shall we continue our tour of the unit?'

He strode ahead quickly and, intent on keeping up with
him, she found it difficult to take it all in, but she couldn't
help admiring the brightness of the new building. What
she wouldn't do to work in a place like this. But not with
Dr Pardoe. That would be unbearable! 'How many rooms
are there for long-stay patients?'

'Forty-five. Fifteen in each triangular pod. There's an
acute wing as well, which has two theatres and an emergency reception room. However, because of staffing cuts,
only one theatre is used.'

They walked down one corridor and Greg showed her a
comfortably furnished day-room—nothing like the shabby
ones found in many English hospitals. The chairs and
settees actually looked comfortable, their clean loose
covers bright and floral.

'I'm very impressed,' she told him.

'Come and meet our oldest resident. Hi, Joe.' He pointed
at Serina. 'From England.'

The elderly man looked confused, so Serina smiled

reassuringly. 'What a lovely home you have here.' He looked up at her, obviously not understanding, but his eyes held a mischievous smile.

'Joe's a Ukrainian settler. He doesn't understand much English.'

Annoyed that Greg had deliberately allowed her to make a fool of herself, she demanded, 'So, how do *you* communicate?'

'We pick up a smattering of the language, and there are always people on duty who interpret.'

Serina noticed for the first time that the notices on the wall were in more than one language. 'It looks as if he's not the only one.'

Greg shook his head. 'It's surprising how many of the older settlers have never bothered to learn the language of their adopted home.'

He patted Joe on the shoulder and led the way back towards the reception area. 'So what do you think of our health care unit?'

'It must be a great place to work.'

'It would be if we had our full complement of staff. As it is, we rely on volunteers far too much.'

'To do what?'

'Assist the residents in whatever activity takes their interest. Painting, handicrafts, bingo—that sort of thing. Even a gardening club.'

'That must give the retired farmers an interest. What do they grow?'

'Mainly vegetables. I expect you've already noticed that flowers don't do too well in our climate.'

His thoughts didn't appear to be on what he was saying so she wasn't surprised when he continued, 'I was just wondering, while you're here would you be interested in working in a voluntary capacity?'

Totally taken aback by his suggestion, she said hesitantly, 'I'm not sure. I'm no gardener and I'm certainly not artistic. . .'

CHAPTER TWO

'I MEANT using your nursing skills.' Greg was quick to put her right.

'I wouldn't mind,' Serina replied, 'but I can't see the paid staff being very pleased if I do that. They might suspect me of pushing them out of a job.'

'I think you're wrong. I should say they'll be over the moon to have your help on a temporary basis. They've all had to take a cut in salary to prevent more redundancies, so they know there's no chance of extra staff in the near future. Someone like you could make life a whole lot easier for them.'

Before she could answer Coral reappeared. 'Sorry, I got waylaid feeding the five thousand. Everyone else was far too busy.'

Greg turned to Serina. 'See. You could be very useful.'

Coral frowned and asked suspiciously, 'What are you suggesting, Greg? She's on holiday, remember? She doesn't have a licence either.'

'I merely suggested she helps us out in a voluntary capacity, that's all.'

Coral shook her head ruefully. 'You would, Greg Pardoe. You don't care who you take advantage of if it's in the interest of your precious patients. Give the poor girl a break. She—'

Encouraged by his attitude towards her, changing for the better, Serina hastily broke in, 'I don't mind. I'd like to help, if I can.'

For some unfathomable reason she cared about his opinion of her, and wanted desperately to prove her competence to him. She was also intrigued to learn more about him. And try to discover what was bugging him.

He shrugged innocently and spread his arms wide. 'See. I'm right. I must go and take another look at Max now, but do try and come in with Coral on her shift tomorrow.'

20

Coral shook her head at his back view. 'Are you sure you don't mind doing this? This wasn't why I asked you to visit.'

'I know you didn't. I don't mind at all, but I don't want to cause problems with the permanent staff. Are you sure they won't see me as preventing more of their colleagues being employed?'

'I'm certain they won't. We all know there won't be any increase in staffing levels at the moment. The budget is overstretched as it is.

'I'm working late shifts Thursday and Friday this week so, if you insist, you can come in with me then and see how it goes. However, I've taken leave over the weekend so that we can do some sightseeing. So don't let his nibs talk you into working then.'

Serina grinned. 'I won't.'

'And, while we're on the subject, I'm sorry he gave you a hard time earlier. He obviously rang his mother last night and goodness knows what she told him. She's a very bitter woman and certainly turned him against her home country long ago. I had a word with him when he left you with Max, and told him that whatever happened between your respective mothers it wasn't your fault any more than it was his.'

'Between my mum and his? What on earth *did* happen?'

'I never really knew, except that Sarah—that's his mother—never mentions your mother.'

'So it'll remain a mystery as there's no one I can ask now. I'd no idea there was anyone else out here from Mum's past. She only ever spoke of you.'

'I think the row was so acrimonious because until that time they'd been good friends. I've always felt that was why your mother didn't visit me. Neither of them wanted to meet up with the other again.'

'You don't know what the argument was about?'

'A man, I believe. Someone they both worked with.'

'What happened?'

'I don't know, love. Over the years I stayed in touch with them both and they knew it. I told them quite openly that, as I didn't intend to take sides, I didn't want to know any details. It all happened years ago but, whatever it was, it didn't make for happy lives for either of them. Your father left when you were a baby, and Greg's father died when he was young.'

'Mum said Dad was an artist so, if Greg's mother panned out the winner, why on earth is she so bitter?'

'I'm afraid it's not that easy. Your mother married Rex on the rebound. He must have soon realised that she didn't love him and moved on.'

'So what's the problem with Greg's mother?' Serina persisted.

'That was the most stupid thing about the whole business. She was already engaged to an engineer, and soon afterwards emigrated to Canada with her husband. So, as far as I know, no one won.'

'It's funny that Mum never said anything about all this.'

'I suppose she wanted to forget it ever happened and certainly wouldn't have expected you to meet up with Sarah or her son.' She gave a rueful laugh. 'Anyway, as I know Greg well enough to say what's on my mind, I did just that. He's usually so laid back I couldn't believe the way he behaved when we arrived today. And, bless him, he hadn't realised just how much he was allowing his mother to colour his attitude towards you.'

Her features lit up with an encouraging smile. 'So hopefully he won't subject you to any more third degrees!'

Inexplicably, Serina found her words disquieting: if Coral knew him that well then so must Heather. Something she recognised that she didn't want to be true, though why—when she disapproved of holiday romances and intended to enjoy the independence that had been thrust upon her—she couldn't begin to understand.

'Anyway, don't forget to keep the weekend free for our sightseeing trip.'

Suddenly conscious that Coral was speaking again, Serina pulled herself sharply out of her reverie. 'It's good of you to give up your leave time to do this.'

'To be honest, I could do with the break and I'll enjoy myself as well. It'll be nice to have someone to holiday with. Ed finds it difficult to get away from the farm. I thought we'd go down to Jasper early Saturday and back Sunday.'

'Sounds good to me. I should think the least I can do is help out on your next two shifts so you won't be too tired to enjoy the trip.'

Coral laughed. 'I shouldn't think there's any danger of that. I enjoy my work far too much. If we're going to be here for the next two days, however, I'll think we'll head for the grocery store now.'

Greg's reception when she arrived on Thursday for her first shift as a volunteer was in total contrast to the day before. 'Good to have you on board, Serina. Before you do anything else, come and see Max. He keeps asking about you.'

Max was seated in one of the day-room but, although the mischievous glint was still clear in his eyes, he looked extremely frail.

'Hiya,' she greeted him cheerfully. 'What's the picture going to be?'

Max laid aside the sketch pad and pencil he'd been using and shook his head. 'Unrecognisable. I promised to try, but it's no good.'

'Is there something else you'd rather do?' Greg asked.

'Not today. I can't be bothered.'

Serina sat down beside him and took one of his hands between hers. 'I'll stay and talk to you for a while. You can tell me what it was like when you first came to Alberta.'

He looked up at her, his eyes suspiciously bright. 'You mean it? Usually no one wants to hear about the past.'

'I do. And I hope you won't mind if I write some of it down. Future generations are sure to want to know, even if this one doesn't.'

Greg smiled benevolently down at them both, then gave Serina a nod and wink of approval and left them to it.

As she had thought, what Max had to tell her was fascinating—details she would never have got from a guidebook.

'We lived in a wooden shack. With just a small range to cook on and keep the chill off. I'd never known such

cold winters before. To get water we melted snow on
the range.'

Once he'd started reminiscing the tales flowed, one after
the other, with hardly a pause. It seemed to Serina that he
was afraid that he wouldn't have another chance. She
stayed with him for a couple of hours—until she could
see that the effort of talking was becoming too much for
him. 'Why don't you have a rest now and I'll come and
hear some more tomorrow?'

He nodded and yawned. 'I could do with shutting my
eyes for a few minutes. But only if you promise.'

'I promise. And in the meantime I'll note some of
this down.'

She made him comfortable in his chair and went in
search of Coral to see what else she could do to help.

Greg caught up with her in Reception as she was trying
to decide which way to go. 'That was a clever move. Max
will certainly be your devoted slave from now on.'

Serina looked at him suspiciously. 'I can assure you, I
didn't do it for that reason. I was really interested to know
and I want to hear more.'

'I can understand that. But you wouldn't have thought
about it if you hadn't been used to working with older
people, would you?'

She shook her head at him, 'I don't understand you. Is
it because I'm English that you don't expect anything of
me? Or—?'

'I'm trying to pay you a compliment, but I'm obviously
not making a very good job of it.'

'You could have fooled me. I thought you were accusing
me of having an ulterior motive.'

'No way.'

Serina laughed at the exaggerated expression of hurt
that accompanied his words. 'I don't believe you.'

He joined in her laughter then, his dark eyes crinkling
attractively. 'I suppose I can't blame you. I have given
you rather a hard time up to now.'

Surprised at him admitting it, Serina met his steady gaze
with a raised eyebrow. 'You can say that again.'

He took her hand in his enormous grasp and, begging

forgiveness with still-smiling eyes, murmured, 'Friends?'

She nodded, too overcome by the warmth of his unexpected plea to speak.

He squeezed her hand in acknowledgement, sending a surge of heat through her nerve endings that took her by surprise.

As he released his hold she raised her eyes to search his face, and was further confused by the unexpected tenderness she saw there. Scared of making a fool of herself, she stuttered, 'I—er—I wondered what else needs to be done. I—I was looking for Coral.'

'She's in the dining-room.'

Serina sped away with relief and spent the next hour preparing sandwiches for tea.

By the end of her second shift on Friday, when she had three sheets of paper covered with incidents from Max's past, she was even more pleased to discover the receptionist had pinned her details onto a large poster of a tree.

The details of every volunteer, together with a photograph and the hours she or he had worked the previous month, were scattered along the branches of the tree.

Serina was rapidly coming to the conclusion that there was an awful lot she could learn from Greenfield, many of them little touches that made life more pleasant for the residents.

Greg came along and gave her an approving smile. 'Great. You're official now. Will you be in tomorrow?'

She shook her head. 'Coral is taking me sightseeing.'

'Where?'

'Jasper National Park, I think.'

Coral's voice behind her contradicted, 'I'm afraid I'm not, Serina. My deputy has just rung in sick. I'm going to have to work this weekend after all. I'm really sorry, love, but there's no one else to call on.'

Greg rested a reassuring hand on her arm. 'Don't worry about it, Coral. I'm off this weekend. I'll show Serina Jasper.'

Coral seemed uncertain about accepting his offer. 'I couldn't expect you to do that, Greg.'

'I'd enjoy it.' He turned his penetrating gaze on Serina. 'That's if you don't object.'

Her blue eyes trapped by his dark gaze, she stuttered an unconvincing, 'N-no, I—I'd like that. It's very kind of you.'

He smiled then, a lazy, teasing smile, 'So would I. I'll look forward to it.'

Serina's thoughts wandered as he returned his attention to Coral and asked, 'Have you booked rooms for the night?'

That smile. The same as he'd favoured the receptionist with a few days before. She'd met his type before. A charmer who, she guessed, didn't mean a word he was saying. Just out for a good time, and no doubt ready to run a mile if anyone should take his empty talk seriously.

'No, we were going to stay with friends. I suppose I could ask them. . .' Coral's voice tailed off uncertainly.

'No problem—we'll take the RV.'

'RV?' The unfamiliar phrase jolted Serina back from her thoughts.

'A camperhome—a mobile home—whatever you like to call it,' Coral explained.

'But—but—' Serina didn't know how to say it but she didn't want to spend a night cooped up in a small van with someone she hardly knew, however attractive he might be.

Coral laughed, obviously understanding the reason for her hesitation. 'It won't be like the Dormobiles I remember back in England. Greg camps in luxury.'

Even so, Serina knew that she wasn't ready for such an experience, not least because she wasn't sure if she could handle being alone with him.

'That's settled, then. I'll collect you early tomorrow.' At the sound of his name being called he turned on his heel and strode away to discover what was wanted.

Serina rounded on Coral. 'I can't spend the night with him like that. I hardly know the man.'

She laughed. 'I'm sure he'll be quite the gentleman and let you have the more comfortable bed!'

'But—but—'

'Just behave as if you're in two separate hotel rooms.

There'll be a partition between you. There's no problem.'

Serina wasn't so sure.

When Heather heard she laughed bitterly. 'I can assure you that Greg isn't looking for any kind of a commitment. We've all discovered that.'

Her injured tone didn't ease Serina's fears—in fact, it did just the opposite.

'I'm not looking for one either. It was your mother who agreed to this trip and I wish she hadn't.'

Heather shrugged. 'I expect you'll survive.' Her tone suggested to Serina that she hoped the trip would be a fiasco.

Which it probably would. Greg was too sure of himself and his looks for her liking, and a danger to someone whose emotions were still vulnerable to anyone showing her the smallest kindness.

He might not be looking for a commitment, but would she be able to resist if he expected a one-night stand?

And what Coral had told her about their respective mothers made matters even worse. Consequently, she tossed and turned throughout the whole of Friday night.

Greg called for her at eight, his sober working trousers and shirt replaced by blue jeans and a whiter-than-white T-shirt which clearly defined his suggestively rippling muscles.

Coral had woken her an hour earlier and loaded her up with an ice-box containing, in Serina's view, enough food for two weeks rather than two days.

'Thanks for doing this, Greg. I owe you one.'

Coral's words made Serina feel that she was a nuisance, so she was relieved when he disagreed. 'Of course you don't, Coral. I was going that way, anyway, and it'll be more enjoyable with pleasant company.'

He lifted the ice-box and Serina's overnight bag. 'We'll see you tomorrow evening, then. Don't work too hard.'

'Thanks for all the food, Coral.' She wanted to say more but felt uneasy with Greg standing by. And, for some reason she couldn't explain, she was glad that Heather had already left for work and wasn't there to see them leave.

Greg led the way out to the campervan and Serina felt

immediately happier when she saw the size of it—it was quite the opposite of the cramped motorvan she had been expecting. She should have known that someone his size would need room to spread.

As he helped her into the passenger seat he murmured, 'I think we're going to enjoy this trip, don't you?'

'Y-yes.' Serina could do nothing but agree, although her apprehension about the weekend wasn't helped by the lazy, sensuous smile that was lighting up his clean-cut dark features.

Averting her eyes, she concentrated on fastening her seat belt.

Affecting not to notice her confusion, he made his way to the driver's side and started the engine.

Having waved to Coral until she was out of sight, Serina squinted through the dust thrown up by the large vehicle's wheels and saw that they were on the road to Greenfield.

'Do you mind if we pop into the hospital for a moment?'

Serina shook her head. 'Not at all. Is there a problem?'

'I'm not sure. Patrick, the doctor working this weekend, doesn't know our friend Max like I do. He rang earlier to see if I was around and asked about Wednesday's attack.

'Apparently he did something similar when the night nurse wouldn't let him stay out of bed at five this morning, but she isn't convinced it was genuine.'

'What do you think?'

'I think he could be playing up, but I'd rather see for myself.'

As he parked the car Serina heard the sound of a siren in the distance. 'Is that an ambulance?'

He nodded.

'Coming here?'

'Where else?'

'I thought your emergency department was closed?'

'Not exactly closed. It's just not staffed on a regular basis, but the staff on the acute wing are all trained to cope. In an emergency we all pitch in.'

As they entered the main door the ambulance screeched up to the hospital and two stretchers were rushed inside.

'What's happening?' Greg asked the receptionist.

'Chap apparently swerved into the path of an oncoming car. Both drivers need attention.'

'Who's down there?'

The girl shrugged. 'Patrick. I don't know who else.'

'I'll just see if I can be of any help.' He disappeared through the door to the acute wing. Unsure if she would be welcome, Serina followed hesitantly.

As she entered the emergency room Greg had started external cardiac massage on one of the accident victims. 'Grab the defib machine,' he ordered when he caught sight of her. 'He's fibrillating.'

Hurriedly wheeling it into position, Serina immediately plugged it in and grabbed the necessary items.

Attaching the leads from the machine to the patient's chest, she adjusted the read-out so that Greg could see it.

As it confirmed his diagnosis that the different parts of the man's heart were contracting irregularly, he ordered tautly, 'Defib.'

Serina quickly applied pads to the patient's chest and positioned the paddles.

'Set to two hundred joules,' Greg commanded.

She nodded, having already done so.

'Stand clear.'

Patrick moved over from the other casualty as Greg administered the first shock. 'Can I help, Greg? That one has nothing that can't wait.'

'We'll get more oxygen into him with a tube.'

Deftly removing the airway the ambulance men had inserted, Patrick speedily slid a tube into the patient's trachea and reattached the oxygen, barely disrupting the supply to the patient.

'No response,' Greg told them, 'I'll repeat the shock—two hundred joules again—stand clear.'

This time Serina saw a definite improvement in the trace on the cardiac monitor.

'Thank goodness—I can feel a pulse. Let's set up an infusion and then try and find out what's happening elsewhere.' Greg searched the trolley drawers for the items he needed.

'His blood pressure's dropping,' Serina warned as Greg initiated the saline infusion.

'Mmm, that leg injury's probably the reason—it's bleeding profusely. Until we can get some blood he'll need a plasma substitute. Can someone organise that?' One of the unit's own nurses rushed away in search of it.

After checking that the young man's neck was satisfactorily stabilised with a collar, a male nurse who had joined them helped Greg to elevate the leg as he applied pressure to either side of the wound—just below the knee.

'We'll do a check X-ray on that leg, but I don't intend doing anything invasive without more facilities. We can always keep it steady by applying traction for the journey.'

The first nurse returned and charted the patient's pulse and blood pressure and noted down everything that was being done.

Having completed a thorough examination, Greg joined her and scanned the paperwork. 'At least his chest seems OK. Let's see, he's gradually stabilising so I think we should get him transferred to the city as soon as possible. What about the other casualty?'

As he turned he let out a horrified gasp and, expecting the worst, Serina turned to look. What she saw was Heather, lying on the trolley—her face contorted with pain and fear. Blood was oozing from a multitude of small cuts, caused by fragments of windscreen glass.

'Hold the fort here,' he ordered Patrick. 'Both these nurses know what's needed as well as I do. *You* can help me with Heather, Serina.'

As Greg gently examined her Heather managed a painful grimace. 'I'm OK—but my arm and leg aren't. They hurt.'

'What happened?'

'I dunno—I was on my way to work when a car came straight at me. From the other side of the road.' The memory of the crash brought tears to her eyes. 'I don't know why.'

'It's not important at the moment,' Greg told her soothingly. With Serina's help he examined her carefully, leaving the neck collar the ambulance men had applied in place. 'Sensation and movement are all fine, but I'd say there could be a break in your wrist and possibly the leg. We'll need X-rays of them both.'

He tenderly examined the multiple cuts on her face. 'Can you find me a dressing pack?' he asked Serina quietly. 'We can remove some of these pieces of glass and try to stem the bleeding.'

When Serina had found what was needed he nodded towards the office, before beginning to painstakingly remove little slivers of glass with a pair of forceps. 'You'd better ring Coral, Serina. She'll be furious if we don't let her know.'

When she returned she took Heather's uninjured hand and smiled reassuringly. 'That looks much better already. Your mum had already left to do some shopping before coming on duty at three. I spoke to your dad, though. He had the handset with him. He'll be right over.'

'Poor man. He hates hospitals. I've always wondered why he married Mum!'

Serina smiled, realising that it was a good sign if Heather felt able to joke.

Coral arrived at the unit at the same time as her husband, but where he was as calm as usual she was panicking. 'What happened? How is she? What can I do?'

'Calm down, Coral—she's doing very well. It just looks worse than it really is,' Greg warned as she approached.

'What happened?'

'We'll get all the details later. Sorting out the injuries is more important.'

'Who's that?' Coral nodded towards the next cubicle.

'Mr Fraser. The other driver. Patrick's looking after him until we can transfer him to the city.'

'What about Heather? Will she go, too?'

'We'll decide when we see her X-rays.'

'*You'll* do anything that's necessary, won't you Greg? I wouldn't trust anyone else.'

'I've already said I'll do the ambulance run because I'm not officially on duty here. Patrick is in charge.'

'I'd rather have you.' The statement came out as a wail.

'Look, Coral, I doubt if anything invasive is going to need to be done. I should be back again this evening and we can review the situation then.'

'Are you going now?' Coral asked anxiously.

'Not immediately. We need to wait a little longer for this chappie to stabilise. And before we go he needs traction applied to that leg. By the time we've done that Heather's X-rays should be through so we'll know what's what.'

While Heather was having her X-rays taken, Serina waited outside and Greg went to see Max.

He was back again before the films were ready, so he joined Serina in the waiting-room and said, 'Max seems fine. I think he was just being naughty this morning.'

Serina laughed. 'I don't blame him. At his age it must be infuriating to be told what to do.'

Greg nodded. 'I agree. There's no reason why he shouldn't have stayed out of bed. We'll have to organise a team meeting to discuss it.' He grasped her hand and murmured, 'I'm sorry about our trip to Jasper, but I couldn't not offer.'

'No problem. I can go another time.'

'I guess so, but it means you've lost one day of your holiday.'

She shrugged and smiled. 'These things happen.'

'Before I leave I'll try and find someone to drive you back to the farm. Perhaps once Ed sees that Heather's OK he'll be returning home.'

'If Coral doesn't need me here couldn't I come with you? I'd see some more of Alberta that way.'

He looked at her thoughtfully for a few seconds. 'That could be quite a good idea. How do you feel about driving on our side of the road?'

'I've done it in Europe, but nothing the size of your campervan.'

'I don't intend you to drive that! My car's in the car park. Have you driven an automatic before?'

This time Serina shook her head. 'But I'm sure I'll soon learn.'

'So, how would you feel about following the ambulance

in it and bringing me back? I can collect the RV then.'

'I'm sure I'll manage that. It won't be a fast drive so I'll have a chance to get used to the car. I'd like to be useful.'

He gave her a lopsided grin that sent her heart spinning painfully. 'You might regret saying that before your holiday's over. I can be a hard taskmaster.'

She laughed. 'But, as I'm only a volunteer, I don't have to do anything I don't want to, remember?'

'Only too well, so I'll have to make sure you *do* want to. OK?'

The sensual timbre of his voice as he made the suggestion caused her toes to curl and her stomach to cramp. What was there about this man that, despite his earlier manner towards her and Heather's warning about him, he could have such an effect on her?

She could only put it down to her emotions being honed to a razor sharpness. Normally she would have no trouble resisting his superficial charisma that attracted not only her but every other female into his web.

'These are the X-rays, Greg.' The radiographer appeared from the darkroom and handed them over with an engaging smile that suggested to Serina that she was another conquest that Greg was unaware of. Or was he? Was he only too aware of it? Was that what Heather had meant when she had hinted that he loved and left?

Greg studied the films carefully, and the radiographer joined him. 'Can't see much in the way of fractures, can you?'

'Mmm—I think I agree with you. Must just be torn ligaments in her leg. And a nasty hole in her ankle where it was jammed beneath the pedal.'

'Let's go and tell her.'

Serina followed him into the room and smiled reassuringly as Greg gave her the news.

'There's no insurmountable problem there that I can see, Heather. So we can keep you here. Let's tell your mum, and then I'll show you my car, Serina.'

As they made their way back up to the emergency department Serina was conscious of Heather watching her with narrowed eyes, and guessed that she was wondering what Serina needed to know about his car.

However, as she was about to explain, Coral came rushing to meet them. 'Well?'

Greg smiled. 'Good news—nothing broken, so she can stay here. Can you find a bed for her?'

Coral rushed off and Greg murmured, 'She needs to keep busy, then she won't worry.'

Once Heather was settled and Coral reassured yet again Greg led Serina out to the car park and indicated that she should climb into the driving seat of his car.

He leaned into the car. 'The most important thing is to make sure the gear selector is in neutral before starting the engine.'

She nodded and moved the lever to the 'N' position.

'Reverse is marked the same as on most manuals.' Although his subtly expensive aftershave, combined with the warmth of his masculinity, was making it difficult to concentrate she smiled confidently and told him, 'There's not much to it, is there?'

Greg nodded and wound the window down, then closed the door. 'Try it out, if you like.'

She started the engine and slowly reversed out of his parking space and did a circuit of the car park, before returning. 'Nice car,' she told him. 'I feel at home in it already.'

'So I see.' He helped her from the driving seat and, keeping hold of her hand, pulled her close to drop a light kiss onto her lips. 'Welcome to the Greenfield team. Even if it is only as a volunteer. *At the moment*,' he added with a deceptively soft voice that she recognised possibly held something more akin to a promise.

CHAPTER THREE

AWARE that Greg was watching for her response, Serina deliberately ignored his remark and asked instead, 'Are we leaving immediately?'

Clearly disappointed, he took hold of her arm with a resigned sigh and marched her towards the unit. 'Only after we've grabbed a sandwich downstairs and then checked on Heather.'

They used the lift to go down to the basement dining area. 'I should think she should be able to go home tomorrow, if not tonight,' he told Serina, 'but she's going to need a whole lot of reassurance.'

'I'm not surprised. It must have been a terrifying experience.'

'I wonder what really happened,' he murmured as they selected their food. 'By the sound of things, it wasn't her fault.'

When they'd finished eating they returned to see how Mr Fraser was. Patrick had organised the traction on the injured leg and the patient seemed more comfortable already.

'All set to go now,' Patrick told them. 'I'll organise the ambulance.'

The convoy left just after three so by the time they arrived in the city the roads *were* quite busy, but when Greg jumped down from the ambulance at the hospital and apologised for making her drive through the heavy traffic she couldn't resist asking, 'What traffic? I haven't seen one jam as yet!'

She had followed the ambulance into the hospital grounds and stopped behind it. Greg lifted a surprised eyebrow at her query, before murmuring, 'I hope you're not proud of your crowded English roads. I hated them.'

'Of course I'm not proud of them,' she retorted, 'but, you know, you Canadians are spoilt with all this space.

Our road planners would think themselves in heaven over here.'

His amusement at her rising to his bait was only too evident. 'Too true they would.'

Accepting his criticism as nothing personal, she acknowledged his agreement with a grin. 'Where shall I park?'

'Use one of those spaces over to the right. They'll know it's my car. I need to go with Mr Fraser and explain all we've done so far. Come into Reception. I'll leave a message as to where to find me.'

Serina did as he'd suggested and, having made doubly sure that the car was secure, she made her way to the enquiry desk.

'Can I help you?' The smiling receptionist rose to greet her.

'I followed the ambulance from Greenfield. Dr Pardoe said he would leave a message for me.'

'You're Greg's driver, are you?'

Amused by the novel description, she couldn't prevent her lips twitching slightly. 'I suppose you could call me that.'

'Why, you're English, aren't you?' the girl enquired with amazement.

Serina nodded.

'I've got relatives in England,' the girl told her proudly.

'Which part?'

'Oh, I couldn't tell you that. They're my dad's cousins. Are you working with Greg?'

'No. I'm over here on holiday.'

'Have you known him long?'

She calculated hastily. 'Three days.'

'And he's trusted you with his car? My.' Her wistful tone of voice indicated that she'd have been over the moon at such an opportunity.

'Where will I find him?'

'He said to direct you to the canteen and he'll join you just as soon as he can.'

'So which way is it?' she asked patiently, aware that

she was rapidly becoming a figure of interest for the bystanders.

'I'm just going for a coffee. You can come with me.' It was a uniformed nurse standing beside her who spoke.

When they were seated with steaming mugs in front of them the nurse enquired, 'You're just over here on holiday, you say?'

'That's right.'

'Are you a relative of Greg's?'

Deciding that it must be a Canadian trait to question so directly, she shook her head. 'I'm afraid not. I've only just met him.'

The girl nodded, as if Serina's words explained everything. 'That figures. Greg can charm the birds out of the trees to get what he wants.'

She drained her mug of coffee. 'It's sure been nice to meet up with you. I have to get back to work now. I don't suppose he'll be long. Have a nice day.'

'Thanks.' Serina watched her retreating back as she made her way from the empty canteen.

Two things were becoming very clear, she thought to herself with amusement. One, Canadians didn't hide their curiosity like the English and, secondly, Greg certainly had a reputation.

He appeared a few moments later, his progress through the canteen punctuated by friendly greetings. He didn't falter in his stride, however, but made his way directly to her table.

Serina felt a suffocating clenching of her chest muscles as she recognised the envy in some of the glances cast her way, but she pretended indifference to the presence of his larger-than-life personality as she greeted him.

'Sorry, Serina. That took much longer than I expected. Have you had coffee?'

She nodded. 'But if you're having one I'll join you.'

When they were both supplied she asked, 'How did Mr Fraser stand the journey?'

'Reasonably well. They're going to let his general condition stabilise before they attempt to do anything with his leg, but hopefully there should be no problem now.'

'Doesn't he have any relatives?'

'His wife is coming up to stay with friends this evening. She couldn't travel this afternoon, but she'll be with him from now on.'

Serina smiled. 'That's good.'

'You like a happy ending?'

'Hmm. Not necessarily. I was just wondering if he was like me. If I had an accident there'd be no one to visit me.'

'I can't believe that. I'm sure you have lots of friends.'

She wrinkled her nose. 'It's not the same as family, though, is it?'

He gave her a deep and penetrating look that seemed to probe into her subconscious. 'I guess not, so let's hope the need will never arise.'

'You seem pretty well known around here.' Unnerved by the sudden intensity of his gaze, she sought frantically to change the subject. 'Have you had other "drivers" before me?'

He frowned. 'Drivers?'

'That's what the receptionist called me—your driver.'

He laughed. 'I see. I trained here so I know most people.' He checked his watch and, raising a rueful eyebrow, told her, 'I'm afraid our trip to Jasper this weekend is out of the question now. So what can I do to make amends? A sightseeing tour and then some food?'

'Sounds good.' Serina smiled.

'Let's go, then, and take a look at the city before it gets dark.'

His touch as he took her arm to steer her from the building caused her heart to lurch painfully, a physical reaction she must learn to ignore if she was to return home with her emotions unscathed.

The wide city streets were almost deserted as he pointed out various places of interest, some of them ornately decorated but none much more than a hundred years old.

'I'd like to show you the rest of the city from the top of that tower, but I think we might be too late this evening.

Finding that the tower entrance was indeed firmly closed, he slid an arm loosely around her waist. 'That's a pity. You must certainly make a trip up there before you leave. Guess we'll have to find some food instead. What do you fancy?'

You choose. I don't know what's available.'

'You name it, I can find it.' When she didn't immediately answer he asked, 'Have you a sweet tooth?'

She nodded. 'Sometimes.'

'In that case we'll drive to the Cheesecake Factory.'

'The what?'

'They serve cheesecakes that are out of this world, and the first part of the menu is pretty good as well.'

He parked the car in a complex of shops and restaurants and led the way towards a building comprising a glass-fronted counter with a restaurant behind.

'We'll have to line up. Do you mind waiting?'

'Line up?' Serina looked around and then, realising that he meant queue, she laughed. 'No problem.'

As they waited she watched enormous slices of a wide variety of cheesecakes being cut, and either sold to take away or taken on plates through to the diners behind.

'I'll never manage something that size,' she told him.

'They'll put what is left in a doggy-box,' he grinned.

When they were eventually seated Serina discovered that the main courses were equally generous, but that no one seemed to mind when she couldn't eat it all and, as Greg had predicted, she left with the remains of her serving of nutty cheesecake in a box.

She found it difficult to keep her eyes open on the journey back. Greg was a fast but competent driver but he didn't talk much, apart from pointing out an occasional place of interest.

'Put a tape on, if you like.'

She shook her head. 'That would really send me to sleep.'

His softly murmured, 'No problem,' accompanied by one of his solicitous smiles, had the opposite effect.

She was wide awake when he suddenly said, 'Look. Over there. Buffalo,' and pointed to his right.

She frowned and then, when her eyes became accustomed to the dusk, she could see movement down in a hollow behind secure fencing.

When it was safe to do so he stopped the car and, climbing out, they moved slowly towards the animals. He slung an arm loosely round her shoulders and whispered, 'Not too close or they'll run.'

They watched the animals for some time before making their way back to the car.

As he started the engine Serina asked, 'What is this place?'

'It's one of our smaller national parks. Popular with weekend backpackers at this time of year. The animals roam where they please.'

'Are there bears?' she asked eagerly.

'Not in these parts. The Rockies is the place for bears.' He turned to her with a wry smile and placed a consoling hand on her knee. 'If I hadn't stopped in at the hospital you might have seen some already today.'

Too sensitive by far to the warmth of his touch, she hastily assured him, 'I'll no doubt see them another time.'

'I do hope so. We'll have to see what can be arranged.'

'Perhaps Coral will be able to take next weekend off.'

'If not, I probably can.'

After just one day in his company Serina wasn't sure that would be a good idea, but as the situation might never arise she didn't consider it worth worrying about.

It was nearly nine when they arrived back in Greenfield. 'I'd like to pop into the hospital and see how things are. You don't mind, do you?'

'Of course not. I expected you to.'

They found Coral chivvying some of the residents along to their rooms after supper.

'How's Heather?' Greg asked her.

'She's cleaned up and much more comfortable. In fact, she was asleep last time I looked in.'

'She's staying the night, then?'

'Patrick thought it best.'

He nodded. 'I'll go and see him.' He left Serina to join Coral, who was helping Max to his room.

'I'm OK now,' Max told them once he was by his bed.

'We'll leave him be for a few minutes. He likes to be independent.' Coral had led Serina sufficient distance from his room not to be overheard. 'Now, tell me how the trip went. Did you manage OK, driving the car?'

'No problem, apart from not realising you can overtake on both sides. I had a fright the first time I saw a car racing up on my inside!'

'I can imagine. Did you see much of the hospital?'

Serina laughed. 'Reception and the canteen. The only places suitable for a driver, I guess.'

'A driver?'

'That's what they called me. I think I'll get myself a peaked cap tomorrow!'

'No one wanted Greg to leave there,' Coral told her.

'So what made him come to Greenfield?' Serina asked, suspicious that it wouldn't have been work.

'He wanted more experience.'

'Experience? But he said that emergencies like today's are few and far between.'

'Thank goodness. It's not acute experience he's after. He believes the quality of life for long-stay patients can be changed for the better. As one of the larger rural hospitals, I think he sees Greenfield as a challenge. And I think the patients are already noticing the difference.' She laughed. 'Look at Max struggling to get himself to bed, unaided. Something that didn't happen before Greg's advent.'

'That's good, isn't it? Stops them becoming cabbages, as they do in some of the British nursing homes I've worked in.'

Coral opened Max's door and asked gently, 'Anything I can do, Max?'

He grinned. 'Leave your friend to keep me company.'

Greg joined the two women at the foot of Max's bed. 'Everything OK, Max? These two treating you right?'

The old man nodded towards Serina. 'Couldn't be better. I hoped she'd come back and see me again. She's my favourite.'

Serina felt her cheeks colouring at his words, but Greg dismissed the compliment to her. 'You're an old charmer. It'll be someone else tomorrow.'

Wondering ruefully if Greg modelled his own behaviour on that of the older man, Serina took Max's hand between her own and teased, 'He's only jealous.'

'You can say that again,' Greg agreed. 'No one tucks me up at bedtime.'

He laughed when Max replied, 'I'm surprised at that.'

'Have you everything you need now, Max?' Coral asked, briskly efficient and, knowing that there were plenty more residents to settle, Serina freed her hand and—after wishing Max goodnight—followed Greg out of the room.

When they were out of earshot she asked, 'Is Heather OK?'

He nodded. 'Now the bleeding's stopped her face doesn't look anywhere near as bad. Patrick is quite happy with her condition so I'll run you home now. You look exhausted.'

'I could wait for Coral,' she offered, unwilling to put him to any more trouble or, more importantly, trust herself to his unsettling presence for a moment longer.

'No way. She doesn't finish until eleven, and not then if there are problems.'

Having checked the room next door, Coral rejoined them. 'Don't wait up for me. I'll probably stay over with Heather, but do make yourselves at home. There's plenty of food.'

'We've already eaten.' Remembering that Ed went to bed early, Serina was suddenly wary of spending time alone with Greg at the bungalow.

'We'll take the RV. That'll save transferring the ice-box and the drinks.' Greg was already on his way out.

When they arrived back at the farm, as well as the ice-box, he produced two bottles of French wine from the camperhome fridge. Ed *was* already in bed but, to Serina's relief, he came out to hear how Heather was doing.

'I guessed as much,' he said equably when Greg told him there was nothing to worry about. 'You youngsters help yourselves. And don't worry about waking me—I sleep through everything.'

To hide her unease as he made his way back to bed Serina took her time emptying the ice-box into the fridge and the cupboard.

Meanwhile, Greg opened one of the bottles of wine and

poured them both a glass. 'To my driver,' he toasted with a teasing smile.

She smiled shyly and took a sip. 'Mmm. That's smooth.' Soon aware, however, that her tiredness was enhancing the alcohol's effect, she decided that half a glass was enough.

He raised his glass, and offered another toast with his eyes. 'I was wrong about you, wasn't I?' he told her.

She shrugged and asked, 'In what way?'

He didn't reply but, instead, reached across and grasped one of her hands. 'I feel bad about ruining your weekend. We should be living it up in Jasper now.'

Her respect for his dedication to work having grown throughout the day, she murmured, 'It's a good job you did. Goodness knows what would have happened otherwise.'

'Patrick would have coped, but in an emergency it's always good to háve people around who know what they are doing. And you certainly do.' He raised his glass again.

His compliment sent a shiver of excitement through her, and she smiled shyly as he murmured, 'You're not too disappointed, then?'

'Don't worry about it. As I said, I can go another time.' She tried unsuccessfully to stifle a yawn as she wondered if secretly he was pleased not to have to do the trip with her.

The thought made her attempt to release her hand but, tightening his hold, he murmured, 'Perhaps we could do a day run some time, taking the car instead.'

Surprised by his suggestion but relieved that he wasn't suggesting they spend a night in the camperhome next time, Serina smiled her agreement. 'Perhaps.'

Considering the signals he was giving out, a day trip was a much better idea.

'Coffee?' she asked as she leaned across to reach the filter jug on the dresser.

Before she could do so he swept an arm round her waist and pulled her onto his lap. With a sweet gentleness that surprised her, he dropped a kiss onto her lips. When she didn't protest he became more demanding, his tongue probing and searching until it found a way beyond the

softness of her inner lips. But still with a gentleness that
aroused conflicting emotions within her.

She knew that this was the last thing she should be
allowing to happen, but she was helpless to stop him. Not
physically, but emotionally. His kiss was releasing some
of the heartache she had bottled up for so long, and she
didn't want it to end.

Even though it probably meant nothing to him, to know
that someone cared enough to show her such affection
was making her skin tingle deliciously. She'd coped for
so long alone that it was heady to discover how enjoyable
it could be, even if it was only for the one evening.

He released her suddenly, then turned her head so that
he could look into her eyes. Ashamed of her response, she
struggled to escape, but not before he'd seen the glint of
tears she was trying to hide.

'You've been through a hard time, haven't you?' He
spoke softly, one eyebrow raised in query. 'Sorry to have
pitched you in at the deep end when you must still be
jet-lagged.'

She rose to her feet unsteadily as in her mind she heard
a mocking voice reminding her, He loves and leaves.

Aware of how his body had reacted when they kissed,
she wondered why he behaved that way when, according
to Coral, he was such a steadfastly loyal son to his mother.

No—it just didn't add up, and in her tired state she
knew it never would. However, one thing was clear—the
sooner she extricated herself from the situation she now
found herself in the better. And yet the sweetness of his
kiss still lingered on her lips, refusing to allow her heart
to believe what her head was urging her to accept.

'I'll put these in the dishwasher and then, I'm sorry, I
must sleep.'

He nodded. 'I must say I don't feel like driving back
to Greenfield after that wine. I'll bed down in the camper.'

She looked at him anxiously. 'Are you sure? Have you
bedding and everything else you want?'

'Of course.' He seemed surprised that she had forgotten.
'We were going to sleep in Jasper, weren't we?'

The start of their trip seemed so long ago that it was

hardly a wonder that she'd made the mistake, but her cheeks coloured fiercely at the thought he might believe she was issuing an invitation.

He must have recognised her fears, as he leaned across and kissed her understandingly on the brow. 'I'll leave a note for Coral and Ed, and maybe see you in the morning. Sweet dreams, driver. Sleep well.'

As if she would, knowing that he was outside and that they would probably meet up again over breakfast.

Surprisingly, she must have slept the moment her head touched the pillow for the next thing she knew was the smell of fresh coffee floating down to the basement.

She checked her watch and saw that it was nearly eleven. She couldn't believe she had slept so late and leapt from her bed to hastily shower and dress.

As she made her way up to the kitchen she was relieved to hear Coral's voice. At least she wouldn't be alone with Greg.

He wasn't there, however, only Coral, who told her, 'Greg is checking on Heather and will likely bring her home later.'

'You'll be pleased about that.'

Coral nodded, 'In some ways.'

Frowning, Serina asked, 'There's a problem?'

Coral nodded. 'Ed's busy with the harvest and I really can't let them down at the hospital. I'm due on duty again at three today.' She hesitated, as if unsure whether to go on.

'If there's anything I can do. . .'

'I know it's your holiday, and you've already lost one trip, but Greg suggested we ask you to look after Heather. He doesn't think she should be left alone and he's officially back on duty tomorrow. Would you mind, Serina?'

'Of course not. I'd love to do it.'

'Greg has agreed to keep an eye on her progress and I'll be more than happy to pay you, so that'll be better than working as a volunteer at the hospital, wouldn't it?'

'Don't be silly, Coral. I don't want you to pay me. You were good enough to invite me out here to stay with you.'

'Yes, but not to work. That was the last thing I intended.'

'I'm enjoying myself just living as part of your family,

especially in such beautiful surroundings.'

'I'd hardly call the farm beautiful.'

'But it's all so different from England. I love it.'

Coral seemed reassured, but when she went out to check how Ed was getting on, and to tell him that everything was working out, Serina remained behind. She needed time to think—time to wonder about Greg. He'd been so keen for her to take up voluntary work at the hospital— that was until her reaction to his kiss the night before.

Flushing red with shame at the thought, she guessed that she knew the reason for his suggestion—he'd seen her tears and had thought that she would cling emotionally so he'd quickly changed his mind about having her under his feet at the hospital. He must have been delighted to find such a convenient excuse.

She wondered if he would be as pleased with himself if he knew that looking after Heather was the ideal solution for her as well. Mainly because she'd sensed his attitude towards her changing. Otherwise the events of the previous evening would not have taken place.

And they were something she could well have done without, especially if all he wanted was a transient flirtation. However enjoyable, it would only bring her further heartache in the long run, which was the last thing she needed.

Her time as a volunteer had taught her a lot and had been enjoyable but, after all, she was supposed to be on holiday, and looking after Heather at home would be a lot easier than some of the tasks she had undertaken at the hospital.

The only person she would miss was Max, but there was nothing to stop her visiting him in her own time.

Greg's decision would definitely benefit her as much as it would him.

Serina was helping to prepare an early lunch when Coral squealed, 'Here's Greg. And Heather's with him.'

She left the vegetables she was scraping and rushed out to greet them. Unwilling to intrude, and more than a little uncertain of Greg's reaction to her, Serina immersed her hands in the water and finished the task.

She watched through the kitchen window as Heather flung her arms round Greg's neck and he lifted her effortlessly out of the car Serina had driven for him only the day before.

As he turned towards the bungalow she saw Heather grimace with pain. However, when the next moment she responded to Greg's attentions with a look of helpless adoration Serina suspected that Heather could be exaggerating her suffering, which meant that looking after the young girl was not going to be the easy option she had thought.

Coral placed a blanket on the giant settee by the living-room window, and Greg lowered his burden gently onto it.

Serina dried her hands and followed them in case her help was needed. But, as the others fussed over her, it clearly wasn't, so she hung back in the doorway.

Greg turned and saw her. 'What do you think of our handiwork? Her face is looking better already, isn't it?'

Serina moved over and smiled to hide the truth. If anything, Heather's face appeared worse than the day before, due to the swelling. 'It's healing well, Heather. How's the leg?'

'Less painful now it's immobilised in a cast,' Greg answered for her. 'I've cut a window in it over the ankle wound so we can keep an eye on it.'

'And her wrist?'

'The X-rays have been checked by a radiologist and he agrees there's no fracture, but it's still giving Heather trouble. I think we ought to support it with a sling. Your department, I think.' He handed over a pack of slings, together with dressings and disposal bags.

As Serina pulled out a sling she thought about Heather clasping her arms around his neck, and silently queried whether it was as bad as she was making out.

She immediately chided herself for the unworthy thought, but Heather's continuous moaning as she fitted the sling told her that her charge was making the most of being a patient.

'How does that feel?' she asked when she'd finished.

'Much better,' the young girl answered breathlessly, before turning wistfully to Greg. 'I think I'd be more comfortable if I sit up a bit more.'

Serina moved to the end of the settee and assisted him to make her comfortable. He smiled his thanks and she remained to watch until the sight of him tenderly brushing the hair out of Heather's eyes sent scorching heat scything through her.

She made a hurried excuse to leave the room. 'I'll get on with lunch as Coral has to go to work this afternoon.'

It was so stupid. Her visit to Canada had marked the start of a new and independent lifestyle which, although she certainly hadn't sought it, she was determined to make the most of.

So why was she allowing herself to become emotionally churned up by a man who, she'd been told, had nothing to offer? Angry with herself, she returned to the kitchen to continue preparing the food.

Coral joined her a few moments later. 'We'll eat as soon as it's ready. Greg may have to go back to the hospital.'

Serina frowned. 'He shouldn't be needed there, surely. Not now both the accident victims are settled elsewhere.'

'I guess not, but you never know what he might have offered to do when he was in this morning. It's a long time since we've had a doctor as devoted to work as Greg.'

That was obvious from the attention he was dancing on Heather, Serina mused drily, but the thought that it was for no other reason than that she was his patient made Serina feel a whole lot better.

As lunchtime approached Coral said, 'I'll go and tell Ed it's ready. Could you check if Greg will eat with us or stay with Heather?'

'I'll have it here and then I can help Heather with hers,' he responded promptly to Serina's question.

'As her nurse, surely that's my job.'

'I can manage today so you have the day off. You were supposed to be wandering the streets of Jasper this morning, if you remember.'

'So were you.'

He grinned. 'I'll have plenty of opportunity in the future. You're not here for long.'

Not wanting to be reminded of the fact, she retorted, 'I could always come again. Actually, if I'm truthful, I'm quite enjoying the peace and quiet on the farm.'

He appeared surprised, and nodded thoughtfully as Serina returned to the kitchen to help serve the meal.

She carried two of the plates through to Greg on a tray. 'Give me a shout if you need anything else,' she told them, before joining Coral at the table.

'Ed won't come in. He says he can't waste the dry weather so when we've finished I'll take his meal out to him. Then we should have just enough time to clear up before I go to work.'

'Don't rush. I can do the clearing up. And take Ed's food out to him.'

Coral smiled. 'Thanks, Serina. You *do* take after your mother.'

An embarrassed flush stained her cheeks as she replied, 'And what about you? You and Ed invited me to stay when you didn't know anything about me.'

'That doesn't mean we expect anything in return. But I will take you up on your offer. I wouldn't mind a few moments with my feet up.' She joined Heather and Greg in the living-room as Serina removed the foil-covered plate of food from the oven and made her way to the field where Ed was working.

It took a long time for the harvester to cross the enormous field, and she feared that the food would be cold despite its covering. However, Ed assured her that it was just right.

After he'd eaten she watched the machine set out on its next swathe, before returning to the bungalow where Coral was preparing to leave for work.

'Anything else you want done?' Serina asked.

'Only find some food for Ed when he comes in. And whatever Heather wants.'

'No problem.' She immediately set about restoring the kitchen to order and made another pot of coffee.

When she took it through to the sitting-room Heather

was almost asleep so Greg indicated that he would join her in the garden.

When he did so they sat in silence for a few moments, though his dark eyes were watching her closely. Eventually he asked, 'Your mother was ill for some time?'

Wondering if his question signalled a return to his inquisition, she replied, 'Unfortunately not. It all happened quickly, too quickly.' She was silent for a moment as the memories flooded back.

Greg rested a comforting hand over hers. 'If you need to talk I'm always happy to listen.'

CHAPTER FOUR

SERINA nodded, but didn't speak.

'What was the problem?'

'Pancreatic cancer.'

'One of the worst.' Greg's sympathy was palpable. 'I suppose she died before you even had time to come to terms with the diagnosis.'

'Yes—especially as in the beginning I found it very difficult to get the truth out of the hospital staff.'

'Even though you're a nurse? That's appalling.'

Serina shrugged. 'Hospitals in England are in a state of flux. The new degree nurses assume more responsibility, but some of the older nurses are still wary of accepting it—they've been conditioned to a subservient role in the past and they are all working so hard that they don't have a moment to discuss the changes that are taking place.'

Greg nodded. 'I know what you mean—staffing levels are pared to the minimum in both our countries and it's the patients and their families who suffer. Which part of England are you from?'

'The West Country. I trained in a newish hospital that hasn't really got itself organised as yet. Which part of England did you visit?'

'Can't you guess? London.' The teasing smile that accompanied his words held an unexpected sensuality that made Serina catch her breath.

To hide her confusion, she nodded her agreement but responded primly, 'We all tend to be judged by London, but the rest of England is totally different. I'm not sure that you have the same phenomenon over here.'

He nodded his understanding. 'Probably because Canada is such a mix of cultures.'

'I suppose so.' Her acute awareness of him made her quickly change the subject, especially as talking about her home still brought back too many unhappy memories.

'While we have a moment you'd better tell me what you want done for Heather.'

'Not a lot. She just needs someone around.'

'What about the ankle wound?'

'Don't worry about it. I'll be in to check it.'

'And the sling? Does she need to keep it in place?'

'It's only there to make her more comfortable. You can remove it if she's happy without it.'

Serina smiled wryly to herself. He'd seen through the play-acting as well!

'Ed sounds as if he's coming much nearer the bungalow. I think as Heather needs her sleep I'll ask him if he can do this bit of the field later.' He rose to his feet as he spoke, but he was too late. At that moment Heather called fretfully.

'I'll go and see what she wants.' Serina jumped up, eager to escape his sympathetic probing.

Their patient didn't seem particularly pleased to see her. 'Where's Greg?' she murmured pathetically.

Serina smiled. 'I thought he deserved a rest. He's not had much of a weekend off so far.'

'I suppose not.'

'Can I get you anything? Would you like a drink?'

'I just wanted company. I hate being alone.'

'I would have thought you'd be used to it, living in such an isolated spot.'

Heather shook her head. 'Someone's always dropping in.'

'Don't you get cut off in the winter?'

She shrugged. 'Not for long. And, if the roads haven't been cleared, we can always get around in Dad's snow-mobile.'

Serina was surprised. 'It only takes a sprinkling of snow back home to bring the whole country to a standstill.'

'I suppose because we get so much we've got the know-how to deal with it. Life has to go on, after all. Where's Mum?'

'She's gone to work. There's only Greg around.'

'Where were you when I called?'

Serina smiled. 'Sitting in the garden, talking.' Her eyes

flashed to Heather's face, expecting a resentful reaction, but she hadn't listened. She was too busy examining her wrist and her leg. 'Is the pain worse?'

The girl shook her head. 'I just feel so tired.'

Serina nodded. 'I'll just sit here quietly and perhaps you'll sleep again.'

When Serina was sure that Heather was sound asleep she crept back to the garden.

Greg was relaxing in the reclining chair. He watched as she took the seat opposite. 'Is she OK?'

'Just tired. And lonely. She wanted to chat.'

He studied her closely, his eyes dark in the shadows. '*You* look tired as well. Didn't you sleep?'

She nodded. 'Too long, probably. I didn't wake until after eleven.'

'So I didn't prevent you sleeping? As you snatch every opportunity to escape my company I thought perhaps I had.'

Embarrassed that he'd noticed, she stuttered, 'I—I—suppose it's—well, I haven't adjusted to the different time zone as yet.'

A cynically raised eyebrow told her that he didn't believe her, but that it was not important enough to argue. Instead, he drained his coffee-cup and then lifted a photo album from the table. 'Coral thought we might like to look through these.' He started to idly thumb through. He gasped suddenly and Serina leaned forward, to see him poring over a full-page photograph.

'Come and look at this.'

'What?' Moving closer, she saw that it was a formal picture of three rows of seated nurses in rather starchy uniforms.

'Do you recognise anyone there?'

Despite having seen a similar photograph in her mother's album, she pretended to study it closely before nodding.

'I *thought* your mother might be amongst them.'

'She is,' Serina whispered almost inaudibly.

He nodded. 'So, which one is she?'

Serina pointed hesitantly. 'That one, I think.'

'I thought so. That's my mother next to her.' She raised her eyes to meet his, watching her intently.

'So they must have known one another. Mustn't they?'

Serina shrugged. 'Perhaps they just lost touch. I know I have with some of the girls—'

'But not with your closest friend, surely?'

'Just what are you trying to say?'

He frowned. 'I'm just puzzled. When you said your mother only knew Coral in Canada it didn't make sense.'

'Well, it's no good asking me!' Serina was becoming increasingly exasperated by him, harping on the subject. 'Can't you ask your mother?'

'I did. The night you arrived.' He subjected her to a penetrating stare. 'Didn't Coral tell you?' He laughed uneasily. 'I thought she would have done. She certainly left me in no doubt that I wasn't behaving very well towards you.'

'She did?' Serina responded innocently.

'I told her I'm certain my mother knew instantly who you were, but pretended she didn't. It's made me very curious, especially as she has always harboured bitter memories about something that happened in England.

'I honestly didn't mean to be discourteous, but when you said you didn't know her I was disappointed. I was hoping that at long last you'd give me the answer I've been searching for, and I did wonder at first if you were holding out on me.'

Serina listened in silence. Did he still think she was hiding the truth, or was he just trying to rest the blame for her dead mother's transgressions squarely on her shoulders?

He didn't enlighten her. Instead, he leafed through the remaining pages. 'Coral tells me that she's kept all the photographs your mother sent her over the years. I guess that's you.' He pointed out a photograph of a leggy teenager in a skirt so short it was embarrassing.

Her cheeks on fire, she murmured, 'Whatever possessed Mum to send that one? It was just a form of protest to wear a skirt that length.'

He laughed. 'I like it. You should show more of those shapely legs.'

The seductive timbre of his voice, combined with the way his eyes slid appreciatively down to the limbs in question, churned her up inside.

Determined not to tangle with him again—especially when there was no one to act as referee—it was a great relief when his mobile telephone rang. Not wanting to eavesdrop, Serina moved away. The moment he finished the call he came into the kitchen in search of her.

'I'm going to the hospital. Patrick tells me Max had another turn earlier, but he's not pulling out of it this time. By the sound of it, he's progressed to a full-blown stroke.'

'Oh, no! What did the tests you were doing show?'

'We still haven't all the results. His blood pressure is definitely unhealthily raised, but we knew that and were already trying to bring it down slowly.'

'Poor Max.'

Having heard their voices, Heather called, 'What's happening?'

Greg explained briefly. 'He hasn't any relatives in this area. I feel as I know him I'd like to see if I can get a response. He took a shine to you as well, Serina. If I don't have any success perhaps you could try.'

'She can go with you. I'll be all right here on my own,' Heather told them huffily.

Serina shook her head. 'Oh, no, you won't. I'm staying. Coral would never forgive me and I wouldn't blame her.' She turned to Greg. 'Did Patrick give you any idea of prognosis?'

He shook his head. 'He said there was nothing more to be done at the moment. He only rang because he knows I'm very fond of the old rascal.'

He grimaced. 'The problem with Max is that he's overweight, he's smoked heavily all his life and, until he came to us, I'll bet he drank heavily too.'

'How old is he?'

Greg laughed ruefully. 'Nearly eighty, so I suppose it hasn't done him too much harm until now.'

'You didn't stop him smoking, then?' Serina asked.

Greg shrugged. 'We suggested he cut down, but it was one of the main pleasures in his life—apart from appreciating pretty nurses! With the older residents we're trying to maintain a comfortable balance—as far as I'm concerned, I'd rather add life to years than years to life.'

'I couldn't agree more.'

'Will you be back, Greg?' Heather asked him anxiously.

He shrugged. 'Possibly. Depends what I find. If not, I'll be over tomorrow.'

Serina walked out to his car with him. 'Do you want her to have anything besides the painkillers?'

He shook his head. 'As I said, the main thing she needs is tender loving care.' He grasped one of her hands and said softly, 'And I think you do too.' He lowered his voice to a provocative murmur. 'When Heather can be left I'll have to see what I can do.'

'I'm fine,' she assured him, ignoring his innuendo. 'I don't know what makes you think I'm not.'

He raised his eyebrows. 'Don't you? I wonder.' He spoke softly and, leaning towards her, dropped a light but questioning kiss on her lips before he clambered behind the steering-wheel.

She was thoughtful as she watched him out of sight. He was so charismatic that it would be only too easy to believe that he really cared but, already aware of his reputation, she knew she would be fooling herself.

With a deep sigh she returned to sit beside her charge.

'Would you like to work with Greg, Serina?'

'I wouldn't mind, but I don't have a work permit or whatever's needed.'

'Yet you helped Greg with that man who hit my car.'

'Only until other staff arrived. I couldn't stand by and let him die because I didn't have a bit of paper!'

'That's why Greg asked me to come over and help with you. And even then he did everything that was necessary. I just fetched and carried.'

Heather nodded. 'I suppose you did. You just seemed so—well—you worked well together.'

Serina smiled. 'That's down to our training. In medicine everyone has to learn to work as a team. We just have to get on with it, no matter who we're working with. Otherwise lives would be lost.'

'I suppose so.'

'Your mum said a lot of social events are based on the hospital. You must do a lot of driving.'

'I drive so far to work and back that I hate taking the car out in the evening.'

'So, how do you get about?'

'Greg usually drives me these days.'

'Does Greg spend a lot of time here?' Serina couldn't resist asking, despite not really wanting to know the answer.

The young girl nodded. 'Mum mothers all the unmarried doctors. She's like me, she loves company and so they all drop in for meals and even just to get away from the hospital for a while.'

'I bet they appreciate that.'

'I guess so.' Heather closed her eyes, making it clear that she was now tired of the conversation. 'Shall we watch a film? Mum's into musicals, but there's other stuff on the shelf.'

Serina ran her finger along the titles. 'What's your favourite?'

'I dunno. Something light and cheerful. I don't feel like concentrating at the moment.'

Serina selected the video of a musical comedy she remembered vaguely from years before but, having settled Heather comfortably before she started it playing, her patient was soon sound asleep again.

She wasn't even disturbed by the telephone ringing. Serina took the handset through to the kitchen to answer it.

'Hiya, honey.' Serina immediately recognised Greg's seductive tones.

'Hi. How's Max?'

'Not good. We can't elicit any response.'

Alerted by the sadness creeping into his voice, she murmured, 'I'm sorry, Greg.'

'Is all well that end?'

'Fine. Heather's asleep again.'

'Best form of treatment there is. You must be bored out

of your mind, though. I wish I could come back to keep
you company, but I feel I want to be here in case there's
any change in Max's condition.'

Was that his impression of her? 'What on earth makes
you think I can't find something to occupy my time?' she
retorted. 'And when Ed finishes combining I'll make him
something to eat, and then do the same for Coral.'

'You don't want to wait up that late. She won't finish
until eleven and you need your sleep.'

Serina didn't bother to argue. 'We'll see.'

Ed was exhausted when he came in from the fields, and
only picked at the food she placed before him. When he'd
finished she asked him to help her get Heather to bed.

As they made their way slowly along to the bathroom
and then to her bedroom Heather complained incess-
antly—until Ed swung her up in his arms and carried her
the rest of the way.

'Good job you're not built like your mother,' he teased.
'Good night, love.' He followed Serina from the room.
'Anything else I can do?'

She shook her head. 'I don't think so.'

'In that case, I'm gonna have a bath and get between
the sheets as soon as I can. Another long day tomorrow.'

'Is it going to be fine again?'

'I hope so—but I can't ever start until the dew dries.'

Serina cleared away the dishes and, having tidied the
kitchen, checked on Heather and then settled in front of
the television to wait for Coral.

She was late and Serina was finding it difficult to keep
awake when she eventually arrived.

Coral took one look at her bleary eyes and said, 'You
shouldn't have waited up, love.'

'I wanted to know how Max is.'

'No change. It doesn't look too promising. Heather
OK?'

Serina nodded. 'She's slept on and off all afternoon.
She seems comfortable.' She hesitated, then asked, 'Are
you on the late shift again tomorrow?'

'Yes, why?'

'I wondered if you'd mind if I took the car and went

to visit Max in the morning. I'll be back in time to look after Heather.'

'Of course you can. I won't need it until after two. If you leave it until ten I should be up to keep an eye on Heather.'

On Monday morning Serina left her patient in her mother's care with guilty relief, and drove to Greenfield. She made her way into the hospital reception, wondering if Greg would accuse her of deserting her post.

He was lounging on the reception desk with Patrick.

'Hiya,' they chorused in unison.

'Glad to see you're not overworked,' she teased. After all, the best form of defence was attack!

Patrick ignored the friendly gibe, but Greg defended them hotly. 'Apart from Max, it's been a quiet day.'

Serious now, she asked, 'How is he?'

'Still unconscious—we're feeding intravenously and the girls are turning him regularly, but there's no change.'

Serina nodded. 'Can I take a look?'

They proceeded to Max's room and the first sight of Max, lying so still, filled Serina with an intense sadness. His eyes had been so alive when he'd told her about his early days in Alberta, and the lack of response as Greg examined him almost moved her to tears.

And it wasn't just because she'd perhaps not hear the rest of the stories. He was a character who'd become very dear to her in just a few days.

She took his hand in hers. 'Hi, Max. It's Serina. From England. I've come again, as I promised.'

There was not even a flicker and she raised her eyes to meet Greg's sympathetic gaze. Seeing a suspicous brightness there, she recognised just how fond of Max he must be. If he felt the same about all his patients it must surely indicate that he wasn't the insensitive person she'd been led to believe, which could explain why his mother's angst caused him such problems *and* why he was so attentive to Heather.

'Keep up the good work.' Greg nodded a reassuring

smile to the nurse sitting beside the bed, and left the room, together with Patrick.

'Do you need any help?' Serina asked the young girl, whom she didn't know. 'I worked here in a voluntary capacity on a couple of days last week. I trained as a nurse in England.'

The carer smiled a welcome. 'Not at the moment, thanks. We turned Max about half an hour ago.'

Serina smiled. 'He certainly looks comfortable. I'll be around for a little while if you want anything.'

She followed Greg and Patrick back to the reception area. Greg greeted her with a woebegone smile. 'Nothing to do but make him comfortable.'

'I guess so. But what about the staffing situation, Greg? I could stay with Max for a while, releasing the nurse in there to other duties.'

'That could be a good idea. I'll go and have a word.'

Patrick called after him. 'While you do, we'll go to the canteen for a coffee.'

Serina watched as Greg performed a double-take. 'Oh, er—all right, then.' His look, which belied his words, made her want to laugh.

Surely he didn't consider her his own property just because they'd been thrown together since her arrival in Alberta? She'd show him. She turned and beamed at Patrick. 'That sounds good. Let's go.'

Although obviously surprised by her exuberance, Patrick joined in the game and grabbed her arm. 'Sure.'

They'd barely settled at a table with their coffee before Greg joined them. 'I've spoken to Kathy, who's in charge this morning. She accepted your offer immediately. So, when you've finished your coffee, introduce yourself to Sue, who is specialling Max at the moment, and you can take over.'

'I'll have to leave about one to let Coral get to work.'

'No problem. I've explained that.'

'Thanks for the coffee, Patrick. When you finish your stint here where will you be working next?'

'I don't know, honey. If it's interesting you want to come with me?'

'Serina's fully occupied at the moment,' Greg broke in sharply. 'Heather needs her when Coral's at work.'

'But not for long, eh?'

Serina shrugged. 'I shouldn't think so.'

'Serina will be needed for most of her time over here, one way or another,' Greg told him heatedly.

Raising her head in surprise, their eyes met and, even in that brief instant, the heat of his gaze was of such burning intensity that she knew she couldn't ignore it any longer. Something was sparking between them that was surely more than just physical attraction.

Recognising how dangerous it would be if she allowed it to develop, she muttered, 'I'll go and see what I can do for Max.' She was relieved that she had an excuse to escape. Greg's capricious behaviour had the potential to cause her far too much heartache.

'Thanks for doing this,' Kathy called to her as she sped through Reception. 'Just a couple of hours will give us a chance to get the routine jobs done.'

She followed Serina into Max's room. 'If you help Sue turn him now, and then just before you leave, there's not much else to be done.'

'Hiya, Max. We're just going to make you comfortable.' Sue spoke to him quietly, but when there was no response she smiled ruefully at Serina. They turned him carefully, talking to him all the time in case he could hear.

'See you later, then,' Sue smiled. 'The call bell is there should you need anything.'

Having checked his charts and his notes, Serina settled back in the chair beside the bed. 'Hi, Max. Remember me? I've come to see how you are.' She took hold of his hand and squeezed it gently, but there was still no response.

The door opened quietly and Greg came in and raised a questioning eyebrow.

She shook her head as he walked to the other side of the bed. When he'd examined Max he indicated that she should follow him into the corridor.

'I think we're losing him gradually. All we can do is let him know someone's there and keep him comfortable.'

Serina couldn't speak in case it released the tears she was fighting to control. She'd never been like this before about a patient. What on earth was the matter with her?

Greg seemed to understand. He placed an arm around her shoulder and, pulling her close, murmured, 'Don't let it get to you, kid. At least he's not suffering.'

She nodded and returned to the room to do what she could, and smoothed Max's forehead thoughtfully.

She was still doing so when Sue came to relieve her.

'Have you had some lunch?' Serina asked.

Sue nodded. 'Yes, Kathy made sure of that.'

'Right. Let's turn him again and then I'll be off to relieve Coral. It's daft, really. I could do her job here, letting her stay with her daughter, but I don't have a working visa or a licence so I'll just have to do what I can as a volunteer.'

'It's marvellous to have your help like this, if only for a short time. Kathy's only sorry we can't pay you.'

'No problem. I don't have to pay for my keep at the moment.'

Coral hadn't long left for the hospital when Heather lifted her head from the pillow. 'There's a car coming.'

'I didn't hear it.' Frowning, Serina stood up and looked through the window. 'It's Greg. Come to check how you're doing. I'll make him some coffee.'

She was apprehensive as she went through to the kithen and switched on the coffee-maker that Coral had left ready primed. Greg Pardoe was looming far too large in her thoughts when she had no intention of embarking on a holiday romance.

He came in through the door without knocking, and as she turned he grasped her upper arms from behind and swung her round her so that he could plant a kiss on her lips. 'I wanted to do that all morning,' he told her quietly.

Determined not to let him see that she felt the same, she moved hastily away, warning, 'Heather heard you coming long before I did.'

He gave her an unrepentant grin. 'She's awake, then?'

'Looking forward to seeing you.'

He made his way into the living-room and Serina heard him say, 'How'ya doing, honey?'

When she followed him in she saw that he was kissing Heather in exactly the same way he had her, and that Heather had slipped her arm from her sling to pull his head down closer.

'Honey'? Hadn't he called *her* that the day before as well? It was obviously a term of endearment he used for everyone and meant absolutely nothing. She'd be a fool to believe otherwise.

'I'm not so tired, Greg, but my leg still aches,' Heather murmured pathetically.

'And your wrist?'

'Oh—er—that's getting better.'

'Let's look at this ankle, shall we? Have you taken your painkillers recently?'

'After lunch.' She checked her watch. 'About an hour ago.'

'That should be fine, then.' He turned to Serina. 'Perhaps you'd give me a hand?'

She moved over and as he carefully removed the dressings she held out a disposal bag.

'It's clean, but deep. If it's going to heal up from the bottom it's going to need packing.' He opened a couple of the dressing packs he had brought with him, before going through to the kitchen to wash his hands thoroughly.

He then proceeded to dress the wound with such a gentle touch that Heather didn't complain once.

'I bet the chap who hit you wished he'd got off so lightly. Apparently he was trying to tune in the radio and took his eyes off the road.'

Heather grimaced. 'Serves him right, then.'

'How is he?' Serina asked.

'Going on well, but it's going to take some time to sort him out.'

When he'd completed the dressing they made Heather comfortable and Serina cleared away the debris while Greg washed his hands.

'That coffee smells good,' he smiled. 'Shall I take it through?'

Serina had already set out a tray with three mugs and milk and sugar, so she nodded. 'Sounds like a good idea. I'll just check if Ed wants his flask topping up.' She rang the number Coral had told her would reach him in his cab and, when he answered, asked if he needed anything.

'Only some company,' he joked. 'This must be the most boring job on God's earth. No, I'm fine, Serina. Heather OK?'

'Greg's with her at the moment. They're just having a cup of coffee.'

'Give him my best. Enjoy yourselves. See you later.' He cut their call and she guessed that he had probably reached the end of a long track across the field.

When she eventually joined Greg and Heather in the living-room the steaming mugs of coffee were standing neglected on the tray, and both were engrossed in a television programme.

Nothing in that, but what did disturb Serina was Greg's arm around his patient as she rested her head on his shoulder.

Serina took her coffee and settled on the other side of the room. When the programme came to an end Heather was nearly asleep. He removed his arm and moved her head gently onto the pillow. When he was sure she was soundly asleep he lifted his coffee and tiptoed out to the kitchen.

Serina followed and the moment she released her hold on her coffee-mug he wrapped his arms round her and whispered, 'When you were upset this morning I wanted to comfort you, but it wasn't the right time or place. So I'm going to make up for it now.'

Determined that he wasn't, she pushed her hands against his chest to distance herself from him, but he linked his hands around her hips and held her gently against him.

After kissing her thoroughly he murmured, 'There's something about you that intrigues me—and I intend to discover what it is.'

She gave a cynical shake of her head. 'Me, and who else?'

He pretended to be hurt by her query. 'Only you, beautiful Serina. You know as well as I do there's something between us.'

'I hadn't noticed.' That was a lie, considering the way he was holding her!

'Why are you so afraid to admit it?'

'I'm not. I just don't believe in holiday romances.'

'I'll have to persuade you, then!' He tightened his hold and pressed his lips firmly against hers with a promise that, as well as reinforcing his words, left her breathlessly unsteady.

As he released her he murmured, 'What a pity I have to get back to the unit today. I don't think you're going to need much persuasion.'

He had clearly recognised her body's involuntary response, not to mention the unbidden flush of sensuality tinging her cheeks.

She moved right away from him then, and slowly opened the door. As he was about to go through he turned and, with a satisfied smile, told her, 'By the way, I think you should know that Patrick is married.'

The statement was so unexpected that she couldn't help herself snapping, 'So? Should that interest me?'

'You tell me.' He smiled again and, raising his hand in a friendly wave, murmured, 'See you tomorrow.'

She didn't move, but watched as he closed the door behind him. Raising her finger to trace the outline of her lips, she wondered at the turmoil that one small kiss could arouse, especially when it came from a man so obviously jealous of her rapport with his colleague.

Then, angrily, she dashed her hand across her mouth to banish any trace of him. She was a fool. He was nothing more than an opportunist, flirting with every female who came within his reach.

How dared he come here on a professional visit and one minute toy with *her* affections, and the next do the same with Heather in a way that Serina didn't consider a physician should behave towards his patient?

She sighed deeply as she recognised that she was overreacting, and why. After all, he was a close friend of Heather's family and a very caring medic. So it was all right. Or was it?

CHAPTER FIVE

HEATHER slept for most of the afternoon, leaving Serina with too much time to think, for—though she tried hard not to let him—Greg dominated her thoughts. And she found her mental images of him increasingly difficult to handle. Especially when she couldn't prevent them churning her insides with an unfamiliar excitement.

To try and divert her thoughts she started to flip through some of the many books about Alberta and the Rockies that she found on the study bookshelves.

As she read more about the area, it had the desired effect. Max's reminiscences began to slot into the history she was reading and, fascinated, she prayed fervently that he might recover to tell her more.

'Where's Greg?' Heather asked the moment she awoke and saw Serina reading on the other side of the room.

'He had to go back to the hospital. Can I get you anything?'

Heather yawned noisily and checked her watch. 'I didn't realise I'd slept that long. Sorry.'

'No problem.'

'Has Greg just left?'

'No—the moment you fell asleep he took off. I think they're quite busy, especially with Max so ill.'

Heather wrinkled her nose. 'I would hate to work there.'

'It's a good job we don't all want to do the same thing. I'd probably be bored doing office work.'

Heather laughed. 'It has its moments. I sometimes wonder, though, if Greg would feel differently towards me if I were a nurse.'

'I shouldn't think it would make an iota of difference, especially if you didn't enjoy the work.'

Heather shrugged. 'I know it's silly, but I get so jealous of all the hospital staff—they have an unfair advantage.

They're with him every minute of the working day.'

Serina laughed. 'They're all so rushed off their feet that I shouldn't think he notices. Anyway, he's paying you enough attention at the moment.'

The girl pouted. 'That's only because I'm his patient. The moment I'm recovered I'll just be one of the crowd again. The more the merrier, as far as he's concerned. You saw what he was like when you arrived at the airport. He seizes every opportunity to chat up pretty girls.'

Serina shrugged. 'He's probably not ready to settle down yet, Heather, and wants to concentrate on his career. There's safety in numbers, you know.'

'I suppose so.' She grimaced pathetically. 'I just wish I could persuade him to see me as something more than Mum's daughter.'

'I'm sure you training as a nurse won't change that, so I should stick with the job you enjoy.'

Heather laughed, but Serina recognised that it was a hollow response. Poor girl. She wasn't that much younger than Serina, but so immature. She really had a bad crush on Greg.

The idea startled her. Was that what she was suffering from as well?

Suddenly wanting to move right away from the subject of Greg, she asked, 'How about a game—cards, or whatever you fancy?'

'I'd rather watch a video. I'm not into games.'

Serina searched out the one Heather wanted and then returned to her books.

As dusk approached she suggested getting Heather along to her bedroom.

'I feel wide awake. Perhaps I shouldn't have slept this afternoon. Anyway, I think I'll wait up and see Dad this evening.'

'What've you two been doin' with yerselves?' Ed asked when he eventually came to the end of his day's combining.

'Sleeping,' Heather replied, and Serina added, 'I've been reading. About Alberta and its history.'

'We've got a lot of books about that.' Ed was pleased

at her interest. 'Grandad came this way some time before
the turn of the century. He found himself a bride on the
way, and when she became pregnant he decided to settle
right here.'

'Sensible.'

'Maybe, but life was hard in those days—they were
the real pioneers.'

'I guessed as much from what one of the patients was
telling me last week.'

'I complain about the harvesting now but, compared to
then, we have it easy. A lot of it was done by hand.'

'The winters must have been pretty awful as well.'

'I guess so. They must have been stuck here for weeks
at a time. Thank goodness we have it a bit easier.' He
shook his head. 'Do you need help with Heather?'

'No, thanks. We've found a way to move her from place
to place.'

'In that case, I think I'll shower before I eat.'

'Can I get *you* anything, Heather?'

'Just a hot chocolate. When you've seen to Dad. Perhaps
he'll come in here when he eats.'

He did, and Serina left them to it until Heather was
ready to go to bed.

When Coral eventually made it home later in the
evening she was exhausted. 'It's been a hectic shift. I
thought I'd never get away. How's Heather?'

'Fine. She's sleeping.' Serina switched off the television.

'You shouldn't wait up. I won't go to bed until the
early hours.'

'I'm not tired—I've had a lazy day. It's a pity I can't
work at the hospital and let you have a break to stay with
Heather.'

'At least I can soon take a few days off. Rennie is
coming back from sick leave tomorrow. Then you'll be
free to get out and see something of Alberta.'

Serina said quietly, 'That wasn't what I meant. I'm quite
happy looking after Heather—I just wanted *you* to have
a break.'

'I know. But it can't be much fun for you here.'

'I'm quite happy. Heather and I have had some interesting chats and I've done quite a lot of reading. I *would* like to go in and see Max tomorrow morning, though.'

Coral shook her head sadly. 'I don't think you'll be in time, love. It doesn't look as if he'll be with us much longer.'

Serina sighed deeply. 'Poor Max. What he was telling me about his early days here brought what I've been reading in your books to life. I know he had much more to tell me.'

'I'm sure some of the others will be just as glad to tell you their life histories.'

'I guess so.' She knew that it was silly but she didn't believe anyone else would make it as interesting as Max had.

The thought made her want to drive over to the hospital immediately just in case she missed one last opportunity to chat with him, but she knew only too well that there wouldn't be one. And that it would be foolhardy to set off at midnight, on roads she hardly knew, when her presence wouldn't make any difference to Max.

However, the moment Coral was up next morning Serina begged the use of the car and drove to the hospital. The receptionist greeted her with a sympathetic smile. 'If you've come to see Max, love, I'm afraid you're too late. He died an hour ago.'

'I see—thanks, Babs. I had hoped—' she shrugged and, struggling to control her tears, walked blindly back to the car.

Before she started the engine she started to read through the pages she had written, following her earlier chats with him, and the words released her pent-up tears.

The passenger door opened. 'Mind if I join you?' Greg's voice penetrated her misery.

She swallowed hard in an attempt to hide her distress and, as he slid a supportive arm around her shoulder, said, 'I came to see Max.'

'I know,' he said quietly, 'but surely you're not going straight back to the farm, are you?'

She shrugged. 'I was going to.'

He gave her a comforting squeeze. 'Max wouldn't expect you to run away.'

'I'm not, I. . .' Her voice trailed off helplessly.

'There are other residents who, I'm sure, would love to tell you about the old days,' he told her gently.

'I know, but I don't feel like it today. Stupid, really. I hardly knew Max, and yet he'd come to mean such a lot to me in that short time.' She inhaled deeply, but instead of steadying her, as she'd hoped, it turned into a broken sob. 'I've never been like this about a patient before.'

'I understand.' He paused. 'Better than you believe.' He turned her head with his index finger to force her eyes to meet his. 'Heather doesn't need you until this afternoon, so I suggest we go and get a coffee. Then, when we've had a chat and you feel better, you can ask Kathy what else needs to be done. Life has to go on.'

'I know. That's why I made myself come on this holiday.' She blew her nose noisily, before turning to smile at him, and gestured towards the papers, 'but it's still sad to think I'll never know the rest of his memories.'

'We'll all miss the old rascal, but I don't feel we failed him in any way. We did all we could for him and he certainly enjoyed the time he spent with us.'

Serina reluctantly held his gaze with her own. 'You're making me feel very guilty. It should be me cheering you up. After all, you've known him much longer than I have.'

'Maybe, but recent events haven't left my emotions raw.'

'You mean they have mine? I don't think so.'

He raised a doubting eyebrow. 'Someone once told me that grief is like a dragon that goes everywhere with you. If you ignore it then it grows until it takes over every aspect of your life. If you pay it the attention it deserves it remains small enough to be easily handled.' He leaned over and kissed her softly. 'I think your dragon is crying out for attention.'

She drew in another shaky breath and said, 'Perhaps we

should go in search of that cup of coffee you mentioned.'

He raised a quizzical eyebrow. 'Running away again?' He paused, and when she didn't reply he sighed and opened the car door. As he climbed from the passenger seat he murmured, 'OK. Coffee. But I warn you. When the opportunity arises I intend giving that dragon of yours my undivided attention.'

As she locked the car he came round and, sweeping his arms round her, kissed her again. But this time with enough pressure to leave her aching for more. Much more.

To hide the desire she was sure must be obvious in her eyes she turned to walk away from him, but he put a detaining hand on her shoulder. 'What are you so afraid of?'

If he only knew that she found him far too attractive a companion, considering his reputation. Especially as she'd soon be back on the other side of the Atlantic.

She welcomed him as a friend for the duration of her stay, but nothing more. And yet, every time he was near, it must be clear to him that her body wanted more than just friendship.

As he caught up with her the memory of his lips on hers turned the tinge of colour in her cheeks to a full-blown blush.

Noticing, he continued, 'You know, a life without love is not worth living.'

She shrugged uncomfortably. 'Maybe, but caring for someone who will be here today and gone tomorrow would be even worse.'

'You have no ties—no lovers waiting for you back in England?'

Ruefully noting that he didn't deny that any dalliance with him would be anything more than transient, she shook her head.

'None? Ever?'

Reminding herself that his direct questioning was just a Canadian trait, she kept her cool and murmured, 'There *was* someone, but when Mum was taken ill we drifted apart.'

He frowned. 'When you most needed support? That

must have been one hell of a relationship!'

Although his empathy filled her with an unexpected warmth she smiled ruefully. 'Not really. We were already on a roller-coaster ride to disaster. He probably stayed around longer than he would have done had she not been ill. I was the one to make the break and now I value my freedom.'

He shook his head. 'But it's not good in the long term. Remember, no man is an island.' He laughed then. 'No woman, either.'

'I'm well aware of that,' she told him huffily, 'but, judging by my recent record, now isn't the right time for me to attempt to remedy the situation.'

'You mean because of Max?' he queried softly.

She shrugged dismissively. 'Amongst others.' She noticed his surprised eyebrow, but ignored it. 'What about this promised coffee, then?'

He sighed and, taking her arm, led her into the unit and down to the canteen. 'I'll get them—find yourself a seat.'

Smiling at a couple of the other volunteers she knew by sight, she found an empty table in the corner.

He placed a filled mug in front of her and seated himself so that he could lean across and, to her embarrassment, rest a hand over hers on the table. 'I wish I knew why you're so scared of relaxing your guard.'

She looked down at their hands. 'I don't know what you mean.'

'Every time we meet the atmosphere between us is so highly charged that you can't have failed to notice. But you pretend not to. Why?'

Raising her eyes to search his face, she saw a tenderness in his expression that affected her more than any words. Although she longed to respond she was well aware that she would regret doing so, and sooner rather than later. It would be different if she could believe that he really cared, but she was sure it was just his bedside manner trying to make her open up her grief to him.

'Heather's doing very well, isn't she?'

Obviously exasperated, he demanded, 'Now, why bring her into the conversation?'

'I was just thinking what a caring doctor you are.'

'I'm not practising medicine at this moment. I am trying to make contact with an attractive girl, but she is not co-operating.'

Ignoring his compliment, she murmured, 'Heather's attractive, isn't she?'

His eyes darkened despairingly. 'Why do you insist on bringing her into our chat?'

'Well. . .' She wanted to defend herself but couldn't, without either sounding petty or repeating Heather's view of him. 'I was just wondering if you knew how she feels about you?' Now, why had she said that? Was it an attempt to find out what he really thought of the girl, or did she genuinely believe that he ought to know?

'I'm aware. . .' He hesitated. 'I'm aware she thinks herself in love with me. But that's not unusual. Girls living in isolation often develop a crush on the first man who comes regularly into their orbit.'

Serina felt shame heating her cheeks. Had her responses made him think the same of her? Resolving to somehow suppress her feelings in the future, she made a start by returning to the subject of her patient. 'So why are you encouraging her?'

'Encouraging her? Why, honey, if I'd been prepared to take her to my bed I could have done so long ago. But I've tried to make it clear to her that I have nothing more than friendship in mind.' He sighed and shook his head despairingly. 'And then you accuse me of encouraging her. Gee—what do I have to do?'

It was at that moment that Serina began to wonder if she was mistaken about him. Had Heather's comments been motivated by jealousy? Causing her to misread Greg's easy familiarity which, she was learning, was typical of all Canadians. And even causing her to mis-understand what the staff of the city hospital were saying?

Closing her eyes in confusion, she heard him say, 'Honey, I wish you'd believe me. I want to talk about you.'

She couldn't meet his gaze, but murmured, 'I'm not sure that I'm ready to do any more talking today.'

His answering smile was wry. 'OK. I get your message.' Suddenly businesslike, he added, 'Let's go find Kathy.' He pushed his chair back and waited for her to join him.

Realising that he'd taken her at her word, she berated herself for being such a fool. Her rejection must have hurt him, and it was too late now to explain.

She thought about Max, and her mother, and the opportunity to unburden herself that she'd just stupidly thrown away, and wondered why the new start she had promised herself was going so disastrously wrong.

Dismissing her maudlin thoughts, she followed him from the tabi and said brightly, 'OK—I'm ready.' She wanted to add so much more, but not to his back view! Explanations would have to wait.

Kathy smiled when she saw Serina. 'Lunch won't be long. Could you help with the feeding?'

At Serina's nod, she added, 'Are you relieving Coral again?'

'Yes, I actually popped in to see Max, but. . .' She shrugged helplessly. 'I'll certainly help with the meals and should finish before I need to get back for Coral.'

'That would be wonderful, thanks.'

Serina moved into the bright dining-room and, having introduced herself, helped to set the tables ready. 'You can help me bring some of them to the table. I'm Wanda, by the way. An LPN.'

'LPN?'

'A licensed practical nurse.'

They walked down the first corridor together. 'We'll start with the two ladies from the far end. They are late onset diabetics and both of them came to us with foot problems. They're healed now, but as neither of them look after themselves properly we intend keeping a close eye on them from now on.'

'Are they on insulin?'

'No, controlled by tablets and diet. If they keep to their schedules it works well.'

Serina nodded her understanding.

'Lunchtime, ladies,' Wanda called as she approached the day-room.

The couple who answered her call were plump and older than Serina had expected, but both smiled broadly as they joined Wanda in the corridor. They were so unsteady on their feet that Serina wasn't surprised that they neglected themselves.

'This is a nurse from England,' Wanda told them. 'She'll assist you down to the dining-room.'

Wanda left her to it and went into the next room.

'What part of England you from?' asked one of Serina's charges as they progressed at a slow shuffle along the corridor.

'The West, nearly into Wales.'

'We have relatives in England, don't we, Mary?'

'You two are related?' Serina asked with surprise.

'You bet—she's my sister-in-law.'

'You're not blood relations, then.' She laughed. 'I didn't think I could see any likeness. Do you know whereabouts your relatives are in England?'

'You bet. They're all around London. Some South, but more to the North. We visited a few years ago. Couldn't get over the traffic and the crowds.'

Her previous experience having led her to expect a vague answer, she was delighted to find someone who actually *knew* where to find their English relatives. 'You're lucky to have so much space over here.'

'You bet. I wouldn't want to live in England.'

They made their way slowly into the dining-room and Serina asked which was their usual table.

'By the window. In the corner.'

Noting the mischievious twinkle in their eyes, Serina wondered if they were telling the truth. However, she assisted them over to the table in question.

But she wasn't at all surprised when Wanda joined them and shook her head. 'You two at it again?' She turned to Serina. 'We try and move them around each day, but these two are determined to stay put.'

'Where should they be?'

'Don't worry,' Wanda laughed. 'We'll leave them unless there's an awful fuss.'

There wasn't, so Serina served the two diabetics their special diets first then moved on to helping some of the others who found feeding themselves difficult.

As they started to clear away and assist the residents out of the dining area Greg came rushing in. 'Have you a moment, Serina?'

She looked towards Wanda, who nodded. 'I'm OK here.'

She followed Greg from the room. 'We've just been packing away Max's belongings. We came across this.'

He handed her a notebook of spidery writing, chronicling some of the events that Max had already told her and some that he hadn't.

She read a few lines and smiled up at him through a film of tears. 'This is fantastic.'

'I'm sure he'd want you to have a chance to read through it properly so I suggest you take it back to the farm with you this afternoon.'

'That would be wonderful.'

'Take care of it, though. Max's closest relative is coming over from Toronto tomorrow to sort things out.'

Serina took the book and stowed it reverently in her handbag. 'I'll guard it with my life. I should have time to make notes this afternoon and bring it back in the morning.'

He grinned. 'So you'll help again tomorrow?'

'If I'm needed.'

'No doubt about that. Even if it's only to soothe the brow of an overworked doctor!' He winked at her. 'Duty calls, I'm afraid. I must take a look at a couple of patients in the acute wing.'

'New patients?' Aware that that side of the unit had been nearly empty the day before, she was interested to hear what the cases were.

'Want to come along and see them?' he asked. 'They were transferred from the city hospital this morning.'

'If that's all right. I don't have to leave quite yet.'

He held the swing door open for her and turned into

the first patient's room, after checking the name outside
the door.

'Hi. Remember me? Dr Pardoe? And this is a nurse
over from England.'

The man seated in an armchair started to rise with his
hand outstretched, but Greg rested a hand on his shoulder
and smilingly prevented him from doing so,

'Stay where you are. How are you feeling after the trip?'

The patient, whom Serina had noticed had a Ukrainian
surname, nodded his head happily. 'I feel good. My wife
comes with a neighbour this afternoon.'

Greg turned to Serina. 'He fell from his harvester and
fractured a hip. We transferred him for surgery and they've
sent him back to us until he's ready for discharge. It's
easier for the relatives that way.' He turned his attention
to the patient. 'The physio will be up to see you this
afternoon.'

They moved on two doors down the corridor, where a
female patient was lying on the bed. 'Hi, Mrs Loziak, I'm
Dr Pardoe—Greg. How're you feeling?'

'Tired,' she answered in a weak voice, 'but glad to be
nearer home.'

She rested her head back on the pillow and closed her
eyes. Greg indicated that they should leave the room.

'Cancer. Ovarian.' He shook his head sadly. 'She
doesn't want to be a nuisance to her husband while he's
in the middle of the harvest so she asked to be moved
back here. She wants to go home but I think she may end
up a case for long-term care.'

'When was it diagnosed?'

'About four months ago.'

'Too late?'

'I fear so. She's made some response to chemotherapy
so we just have to wait and see if it continues.'

'Poor soul.'

He nodded regretfully. 'That's the way it goes, isn't it?'
His eyes, full of sympathy, held hers for a long moment
and she knew that they were both thinking about her
mother and that he'd been right. She did want to talk about
it but guessed that, after her earlier refusal, he wasn't

risking another rebuff. Instead, he murmured politely, 'If you'll excuse me I must search out the nurse who's looking after these two.'

'And I must see Kathy and then get back to Heather.' She was desolate as she made her way from the acute wing back to the reception area. Greg made no attempt to hide the fact that he cared about people, whether friends or patients. She hoped she hadn't thrown away the right to be included amongst them.

When she eventually left the unit, however, he'd reverted back to the Greg she knew. He gave her a warm smile amd told her, 'I'll be along to see Heather later, OK?'

'Yes—certainly.' Her confidence boosted by the warmth of his greeting, she grinned mischievously. 'I'm sure she's looking forward to that.'

'What about you?'

Pretending not to understand, she wrinkled her nose. 'I'll be there.'

'I wanted to know if you were looking forward to my visit,' he persisted.

'What do you think?' she teased, and skipped down the steps to the car park.

He shook his head as he watched the jaunty swing of her hips. What a change in her manner since that awful moment she'd arrived to discover that Max was dead. When he'd found her in the car his first intention had been to cheer her up, and he'd succeeded. Until he'd been so sure that she would welcome the opportunity to talk things over with him that he'd pressed too hard, causing her to clam up on him.

She was so different from any girl he'd ever met before that he couldn't bear to think she was unhappy inside and he was doing nothing about it. She was probably the kind of girl he would have married, if it were possible. But it wasn't. If he loved someone enough to want to marry them there was no way he was prepared to do so and put them at risk of being left alone to bring up a family.

As his mother had had to. He'd seen her struggle and become increasingly bitter.

The trouble was that, as a doctor, he knew too much. Despite all the modern advances and all the precautions he could take with diet and exercise, with his family history there was still a good chance that he would suffer a fatal heart attack before he was forty. Hadn't it happened to that bright new consultant they'd appointed to the city hospital? And if anyone was a fitness freak he was. Yet it hadn't saved him.

No, he had nothing permanent to offer any girl, but while Serina was over in Canada he could at least offer her his friendship. He'd like to show her his country, as much of it as he had the time for, but that's as far as it would go.

A girl like Serina, who'd been through such a hard time recently, didn't need another crisis in her life so he would try and hide his feelings and just give her a holiday to remember.

It wouldn't be easy, though. He already found her far too attactive but hopefully—with her over here for such a short time—there should be no harm done, and perhaps he'd be able to help her overcome the traumas she'd already suffered.

When he arrived at the farm he dropped a kiss lightly on Serina's brow and said loudly, for Heather's benefit she was sure, 'Rennie is back from sick leave so Coral is taking the day off on Thursday to be with Heather. I've asked Patrick to stand in for me. We can make our delayed trip to Jasper that day. How does that sound?'

Not wanting to hurt him again, Serina didn't hesitate. 'It sounds great, Greg, but I'm not sure about walking out on Coral like that. She deserves a rest, rather than looking after another patient at home.'

Greg laughed and closed the kitchen door so that Heather couldn't overhear. 'You know jolly well that looking after Heather can't be compared to the hard work at the unit!'

Pretending to take umbrage, Serina retorted, 'So you're

implying that I do nothing all day, are you?'

He laughed even louder then, placing a finger to his lips, whispered, 'I didn't mean you've been doing nothing, but I can tell you she won't play her mother up like she's been doing you.'

Serina muttered indignantly, 'Now you're insinuating that I'm not coping properly with my patient.'

'Of course I'm not.' He was suddenly serious. 'But I'm well aware that Heather can be a little minx when she chooses.'

'And yet you encourage her.'

'How d'ya mean?'

'Like I said before, I don't consider that a good bedside manner includes putting your arm around a patient.'

'Depends on the circumstances.' He slid an arm along her shoulder, pulling her closer before murmuring, 'You're not jealous, are you?'

When she didn't answer he hesitated, then continued, 'You've been through a difficult time recently and I think that, combined with your English reserve, is distorting your judgement.'

Was he trying to tell her not to get the wrong idea about him as well? If so, he needn't bother. She was only too aware of his reputation to lose her heart to him.

'So, are you on for Thursday?'

'If Coral doesn't mind.'

'I know she won't. She's already said so. If we're to see much, though, it'll mean a very early start. And this time we won't call in at the hospital, I promise.'

'Good.' Her reply was cool. He might have asked her first, before discussing it with Coral. As he hadn't, and in the light of what he'd just said, she could only guess that he felt obliged to suggest a repeat outing because she had been deprived of the previous one by his actions.

'I'll collect you around five, then, and do tell Coral she's to have a lie-in—we're perfectly capable and we won't need food. I'll make other arrangements.'

When he went through to see Heather Serina hugged herself in total confusion. When she'd accepted Coral's invitation she'd hoped to see something of Canada. To do so in the company of a man as attractive as Greg was a bonus.

But it wasn't one that would be easy to handle because every time he was near his musky masculinity set every nerve ending in her body jangling.

CHAPTER SIX

EVENTUALLY regaining her composure, Serina followed Greg into the lounge. 'Do you want help with the dressing?'

He broke off his chat to Heather and smiled warmly. 'Of course. What else would I expect of her private nurse?'

After their earlier exchange she responded in the same vein. 'What else, indeed! I've done nothing so far today!'

He grinned and raised Heather's leg to assist Serina in removing the dirty dressing. When the wound was exposed he smiled. 'Fantastic. That's healing incredibly well, Heather. We'll redress it today with a little packing, but by tomorrow a dry dressing will probably suffice.'

'Will you remove the plaster cast, then?' the young girl asked eagerly.

'I think we might leave that for a few more days to give the ligaments a chance to heal, but you can start getting around on it now. But not until you have the proper boot to protect the cast. I'll send one home with Coral tonight.'

Heather smiled and swung herself round so that she could rest both feet on the floor. 'I can't wait to be able to move about on my own.'

'By the way, how's your arm?' Greg asked her, winking almost imperceptibly at Serina.

'No problem now. I haven't worn the sling at all, have I?' she appealed to her nurse.

Trying to suppress a grin, Serina shook her head. 'That was because you were able to support the arm while you were resting.' She gathered up the dirty dressing bag and left the room to dispose of it. Greg followed her almost immediately.

'I told you she was playing you up,' he whispered.

'Good job I didn't allow her to get away with it, then,' she murmured archly.

His light kiss clearly acknowledged that she was right.

When they returned, to find Heather immersed in yet another TV soap opera, Greg frowned and suggested, 'I don't have to be back at the unit until later this afternoon. How about I take you both for a short trip out? We could show you another bit of Alberta, Serina, and a breath of fresh air won't do you any harm, Heather.'

Heather wrinkled her nose disdainfully but Serina said, 'That sounds nice.'

'We could motor over to Vegreville,' Greg suggested.

'Vegreville?' Serina queried.

'A few shops and an uninteresting egg-shaped monument,' Heather told her scornfully.

'It might be uninteresting to you, but I'm sure Serina would like to see it,' Greg retorted sharply. 'This is her holiday, after all.'

Ignoring the rebuke, Heather reluctantly switched off the TV and allowed herself to be helped out to the back seat of the car. 'You'd better ring Dad,' she told Serina, 'then he can keep an eye on the house.'

Having done as she suggested, Serina took her place in the front passenger seat and picked up a map.

'We're heading for Highway 16,' Greg told her.

The area was so sparsely populated that she found it easily. 'It's quite a journey.'

Greg shrugged. 'Not for Canada.'

She tried to convince herself that the strange contentment she felt was due to escaping the one-to-one care of Heather. A stealthy look at Greg's profile, however, left her feeling as if she'd been punched in the midriff. Already conscious that his presence usually played havoc with her emotions, the fact that he was doing this trip for her benefit left her barely able to control them.

As his car rapidly swallowed up mile after mile of prairie road he pointed out some original homesteads that were still standing but, though they passed through several small communities, there was little else of interest to see until they reached the outskirts of a sizeable town.

'This is it—Vegreville,' he told her with a grin as he swung the car into the parking lot of a community park.

'And there's the Pysanka—the largest Easter egg in the world.'

'It's beautiful,' Serina breathed, climbing from the car. 'I'll help you out, Heather.'

'Don't bother,' the girl muttered petulantly. 'I've seen it before—often.'

Greg grinned and teased, 'Don't go away. We won't be long.'

As they walked towards the monument and saw the sun glinting on the hundreds of shaped metal panels Serina asked him, 'What is it for?'

'It marks the Mounted Police keeping the peace in Alberta for a hundred years.' He waited until she had taken several photographs. 'It was designed by computer. The interpretive notices tell you all about it. Take your time reading them. I'll go back and chat to Heather.'

When she returned to the car Greg had procured three cans of Coke. 'Thirsty work this sightseeing,' he told her as he handed her one.

'It's fantastic. I've learnt quite a lot more about the Ukrainian settlers.' Serina's blue eyes were alight with enthusiasm but, although Greg smiled his agreement, Heather remained sullen.

'Anywhere you'd like to go?' Greg asked her.

'Not until I can get around the shops.'

'Hopefully, that shouldn't be long,' he told her, raising a resigned eyebrow in Serina's direction.

He delivered them safely home, but refused refreshment as he had to get back to the unit.

Serina followed him to the car and handed him back Max's diary. 'Thanks for letting me see it. I've made notes of the more interesting bits.'

'Good. I'm sorry I can't let you keep it, but it's not mine to give away.'

'No problem. I'm grateful at having the chance to read it. Anything else you want done for Heather?'

He shook his head. 'Once she's got the boot she can start being mobile and can look after herself. She's lucky. She has youth on her side.'

'Thanks a million for the outing, Greg. It was great and

I'm sure the change of scene will have done Heather good, however much she hated it!'

He smiled and pulled her into his arms. 'You're doing a great job under difficult circumstances. Don't think I haven't noticed. That's why I wanted to give you a break.'

He kissed her then, before holding her at arm's length so that he could scrutinise her with dark eyes so full of appreciation that Serina felt that her knees would give way at any moment.

'I'm sorry, love, I have to go,' he whispered as he crushed her to him and kissed her again. Then he released her reluctantly and drove away, leaving her feeling like a limp rag.

Unable to move immediately, she watched him out of sight—her thoughts tearing at her heartstrings. His distrust of all things English and his reluctance to settle with just one woman, not to mention the fact that she was in Alberta for such a short time, surely made it impossible for their obvious physical attraction to develop into anything more.

Chiding herself for her foolishness, she rejoined Heather who had brightened immeasurably at the sight of her TV.

Coral arrived home earlier than expected. 'It's been quiet this evening.' She handed Heather the plaster boot. 'Greg says you're to take it easy—don't go rushing around. He'll be in to see how you're managing tomorrow.' She turned to Serina. 'I'm taking the next three days off, so Kathy asked if you'd be free to help tomorrow? I told her you were going to Jasper on Thursday, but she said a few hours tomorrow would be wonderful.'

'On the evening shift?'

'No, she said you'd be most useful in the morning.'

'No problem.'

'Greg said if you were in in the morning you could tell Max's nephew about your notes.'

She nodded thoughtfully. 'And perhaps I'll find another resident who can fill in some of the gaps. Er—will it be all right—?'

'Take the car,' Coral offered, reading her mind.

'If you're sure you won't need it yourself.'

'I'll be here with Heather. And there's always Ed's truck in an emergency.'

To her disappointment, Greg was nowhere in sight when she arrived at the unit the next morning so Serina reported to Kathy. 'What would you like me to do?'

'Would you mind helping Wanda with the baths and beds?'

'Not at all. I'll meet more of the residents that way.'

'Only until ten. Max's nephew is coming at that time and Greg has asked if you can join them.' She appeared puzzled. 'I don't know why.'

'It's because I chatted to Max about his early days out here. I'm hoping to put it all down for future generations. Greg thinks his relatives would like to know what I intend to do.'

Kathy nodded. 'That's the reason, is it? What a pity you didn't get to know Max earlier, in that case.'

'He'd written quite a few notes himself. Greg let me read them through yesterday. And perhaps I'll find other patients willing to add their recollections.'

'I'm sure you will. They all like to talk about their past but, at our present staffing level, it's difficult to find the time to listen.'

'Perhaps that's something I can help with.'

'Would you rather do that than help Wanda?'

'Oh, no, I can do both.' She smiled to reassure Kathy, who she could see was uneasy about asking Serina to do nursing work when she couldn't pay her. 'I don't mind what I do at all.'

Kathy came in search of Serina at ten. 'Greg's waiting for you in his office.'

A stomach-churning excitement filled her at the thought of seeing him again, despite knowing that it was for no other reason than to meet Max's nephew.

'Hi, come in.' Greg answered her knock.

She opened the door and saw that he was alone. 'He's not arrived yet?'

Greg shook his head as a tray of coffee was brought in. 'I thought we could share a coffee while we waited.'

'Sounds nice, but I don't see why you want me here.'

'These meetings are never easy. I thought if you told him about the notes you've made it might help.' He quirked an eyebrow. 'All ready for tomorrow.'

'I haven't given it a thought.' What a liar she was becoming!

His eyes searched her face relentlessly and she knew that he didn't believe her.

'Well, be ready at five. I don't want to wake the whole house.'

'I'll be waiting,' she assured him and then wondered why the look that flashed across his face was one of relief. Had he expected her to back out at the last minute?

A knock on the door left her no time to ponder further. Greg shot to his feet and, opening it, greeted Max's nephew warmly.

'Call me Bud,' the cheerful middle-aged man told them as he shook both their hands in turn.

'This is Serina Grant. She's a nurse from England, and had become very fond of your uncle.'

Serina nodded. 'He told me some fascinating tales of his early days out here, and I've written them down. I wish there'd been time to hear more, but he'd made notes of his own and Dr Pardoe let me look through them.'

'Great! You making them into a book?'

'I'd like to, for Max's sake. But it won't be a book— there's only enough for a small pamphlet.'

Bud handed over a business card. 'Gee, that would make me real proud. I'd like to see a copy some time.'

Serina smiled. 'I'll certainly send you one if it materialises.'

A beaming smile lit up his face. 'And give me a shout if I can help some more. I'll keep these notes safe. Call if you need information, won't you?'

'I will, thank you.'

While they were talking Greg had refilled the coffee-cups and handed a fresh one to Bud. 'When we've finished these would you like to see your uncle?'

Bud hesitated. 'I guess so but, you know, I hardly ever saw him alive. We lived just too far apart.'

Serina experienced a pang of sadness as she recognised just how lonely Max must have been until he was admitted to the unit. How warm and welcoming it must have seemed to him after his solitary existence.

Her eyes encountered Greg's sympathetic glance and she wondered if he was remembering her saying that she would have no one to visit her.

Swallowing hard, she murmured, 'You don't need me any more, do you? I ought to go and finish the beds.'

Greg gave her a warm smile. 'Thanks, Serina.'

'Yes, thanks, Nurse. Don't forget to keep in touch.'

She closed the door behind her with a deep sigh. He hadn't really needed her there. He could have told Bud what she was going to do just as easily. So why had he insisted that she join him? Surely he didn't need an excuse to invite her for coffee? Or did he? Was it his way of keeping his distance, while still enjoying her company? If so, the thought of their trip to Jasper the next day was making her increasingly uneasy.

When he called for her at five on Thursday morning a fine drizzle soaked Serina as she crept out to join him.

'Sorry about the weather,' he murmured as he took her bag and assisted her into the passenger seat. 'I did order the sun but something seems to have gone wrong.'

'I'm relieved to know that you don't get *everything* right,' she teased nervously.

As he was about to close the car door he leant back in and, shaking his head as if unable to believe what he'd heard, he told her, 'I get most things I want. And I'll prove it!'

As he leaned towards her she suspected that he was going to extract revenge for her taunt so she added hastily, 'Perhaps it'll dry up later.' She realised too late that he'd been about to kiss her, and when he withdrew with a rueful grimace she felt a pang of disappointment.

'I can wait—and not only for the sun!' His comment as he climbed into the driving seat was accompanied by a mischievous smile.

A shiver of anticipation scudded down her spine as she

waited for him to elaborate. He didn't but, starting up the car, bantered, 'Hey, what am I doing, discussing the weather like an Englishman?'

She laughed. 'Perhaps you're turning into an Anglophile.'

'You could be right.' The glance he shot towards her told her that he was as surprised as she was at the concept.

She relaxed back in her seat with an increasing optimism about the day ahead. The events of the previous Saturday had actually done her a favour. She'd hardly known him then so all kinds of problems might have arisen. At least she was forewarned today.

As they left prairie country and sped through the quiet city she asked, 'How long till we reach Jasper?'

'Depends. If we stop for breakfast we should get there around ten. Then our time's our own, which it wouldn't have been last weekend.'

She was surprised. 'Why?'

'I was supposed to meet up with somebody on Saturday.'

'Business? Or pleasure?'

He laughed. 'Now you're asking questions like a true Canadian!'

She felt the heat flare in her cheeks and murmured, 'Sorry. It's none of my business.'

He rested a hand over hers on her lap. 'If I'm turning into an Anglophile there's no reason why you shouldn't become more like us,' he appeased. 'As it happens, I'd arranged to meet up with a friend who is working in the hospital at Jasper. He doesn't know I'm coming today.'

Surprised and if the truth be known, not displeased to learn that his harem didn't extend as far as Jasper she offered generously, 'I don't mind if you still want to meet up. I can amuse myself.'

'If I do that we might be expected to join him for a meal this evening, and I'd rather have you all to myself today.'

To hide the pleasure she felt at his words, she asked, 'Is Jasper a large town?'

'Not really, but bigger than Greenfield with a population swelled by tourists and itinerant youngsters.'

'Does that cause problems?'

'The usual. Drugs and an escalating AIDS problem.'

'Inevitable, I guess. Would you like to work there?'

'I don't think so. I like the prairie people. I don't think I'd be so sympathetic with youngsters whose lifestyle is making them ill.'

Serina raised an eyebrow wryly. 'I noticed quite a few of your present patients have hit the bottle in the past, and many are still smoking.'

He laughed. '*Touché*. But they're just easier to deal with than the youngsters! They don't answer back!'

'I wouldn't say that's true of any of our patients back home!'

'Careful. You're giving me second thoughts about your country!'

'In that case, I'd better change the subject pretty smartly!'

He laughed, a trifle uneasily she thought, and— concentrating on the road ahead—said nothing more.

Serina was baffled. Surely he hadn't taken her throwaway comment to mean that she was hoping he would visit her in England?

Uncomfortable with the silence, she sought in vain for something to say that wouldn't destroy the empathy that had been between them at the start of the journey.

Unable to bear it any longer, she blurted out, 'It's good of you to give up your day to show me an area you must have seen many times before.'

'It's not good of me at all. I don't have the time to visit the Rockies as often as I'd like.' He rested a hand gently on her knee. 'And to see them in the company of an attractive Englishwoman has to be a bonus. I hope you appreciate them as much. Over the years I've discovered that not everybody does.'

His reply burst Serina's foolish bubble of optimism as he made it clear that she wasn't the first he'd brought here. He'd obviously sensed a need to warn her once again not to expect too much from him. 'I hope so too,' she joshed. 'After such a build-up it'll be a disappointment if I don't.'

'I'm sure you will.'

Deciding that there was nothing else she could usefully add, she watched the breaking dawn without speaking. After a few moments he started a cassette playing.

Serina was entranced by the music. It was a blend of animal sounds, birdsong and gentle instrumental music, some of it played on a harp. She found it very relaxing— until the sound of trickling water turned her thoughts to a comfort stop!

'What is this tape?' she asked him eventually.

'It's called ''The Rocky Mountain Suite''—there's a whole series of them.'

'It's lovely—so different.'

He grinned. 'I thought you might like it—they're produced with tourists in mind.'

Determined to give as good as she got, she raised an eyebrow. 'And yet you have one in the car?'

'I told you I can't get enough of the Rockies,' he told her brusquely. 'I'm a tourist there, don't forget.'

Aware that he knew she'd read his meaning wrongly, she nodded guiltily. 'I suppose you are. I hadn't thought of it that way.' She settled back in her seat to listen to the remainder of the tape as they sped along the tree-lined road.

She was surprised when he suddenly indicated a right turn. Aware that they were already on the road to Jasper, Serina queried, 'Where to now?'

He brought the car to a standstill beside a service station. 'Comfort stop and a fill-up for the car.' He climbed out and stretched lazily, before coming round to Serina's side of the car.

'Somebody heard my request after all,' he grinned. 'It's stopped raining.'

Relieved that his good humour had returned, she acknowledged his triumph with a smile.

Food was available in a diner attached to the service station. The moment they were seated the mugs on the table in front of them were turned the right way up by the waitress, and filled with coffee.

'Nectar! That's what I call service,' Serina told him.

He laughed. 'Of course, you've only sampled the hospital canteen to date. This is standard practice over here. *And* you can have as many refills as you want! Something that doesn't happen in London, I discovered.'

'Too true.'

They drank their coffee in silence, allowing Serina to study the menu.

'Eggs and bacon with pancakes and hash browns? Or will you join me in boiled eggs and wheatmeal toast?'

Surprised again by his rigid adherence to a healthy diet, she murmured, 'I'll join you, I think. I'm not into fried breakfasts.'

When they'd given their order he looked at her with laughter in his eyes. 'I was secretly dreading having to watch you enjoy hash browns!'

'You are careful about what you eat, aren't you?' she probed tentatively. 'And Heather tells me you work out at the gym regularly. Are you in training for something special?'

He shrugged evasively. 'Just life. I try to be sensible. I suppose I've seen too much illness caused by unhealthy lifestyles.'

She didn't somehow believe that he was telling her the whole story but, as she couldn't imagine why and the breakfast had arrived, she dismissed the thought.

'Refill?' The waitress was hovering with a jug of coffee.

'Please.' She nodded.

Over their second coffee she asked Greg, 'Which part of Canada are you from?'

'I was born near Calgary.'

'Is your home still there?'

He shook his head. 'My mother has moved frequently since Dad died. At the moment she's part-owner of a store that sells dinosaur souvenirs in the Badlands. It's not doing very well, so she'll probably soon move on again.' He hesitated. 'She seems unable to settle.'

'The Badlands? What——?'

'The Alberta Badlands. East of Calgary. Haven't you heard of them?'

'I did read something about them in one of Coral's

books, but wasn't sure what or where they are.'

'Rather than try to describe a landscape that's impossible to visualise until you've seen it, I'll take you there one day.'

Her heart gave a sudden lurch at him suggesting another outing. 'I—I'd like that.'

He seemed amused by her hesitancy and his smiling eyes held her gaze for a long time, leaving her even more confused. Surely such an offer contradicted totally what she believed he'd been trying to tell her earlier?

'Let's hit the road again,' he said at length.

She nodded.

The highway was almost empty so Greg was able to move the gears into cruise control and relax back in his seat. It was at that moment that Serina saw a spectacular range of mountains appearing ahead of them, some showing traces of snow and others with cloudy cobwebs trailing across their peaks.

'Is that the Rockies?'

He nodded.

'It's—it's incredibly beautiful,' she breathed. 'I never imagined anything like this.'

He turned to her with a satisfied grin. 'And that's only the start! It's impossible to overdo the superlatives.'

Serina started to answer him but a lump in her throat prevented her speaking. Instead, she felt tears pricking her eyelids and raised a hand to wipe them away.

Greg appeared to understand. He reached across and rested a warm hand firmly on hers.

'I know exactly how you feel, kid, and I'm glad you do. This area still affects me the same way.'

She dabbed at her eyes with a tissue, then murmured, 'Canada's having the weirdest effect on my emotions. I seem to cry at everything since I've been here.'

He inhaled deeply. 'I don't think you can entirely blame the country for that.'

She knew she couldn't. It was Greg turning her emotions inside out, but that was the last thing he would want to hear.

Soon after they entered the Jasper National Park he

stopped to point out mountain goats on the side of the road.

'If you see cars parked by the roadside in the parks it usually means there are animals to be seen.'

She retrieved her camera from the bag he'd placed in the back of the car and took a couple of photographs.

He laughed. 'You'll run out of film if you take two of every animal we come across.'

Almost immediately she saw an elk, grazing at the side of the road. At her cry of excitement he stopped the car, but as she climbed out warned, 'Don't get too close. It's a male and they can be unpredictable in the mating season.'

'Like men,' she murmured to herself. 'Unpredictable.'

When, eventually, she climbed back into the car he told her, 'It's not far to Jasper now and, unless the rangers have rounded them up recently, you'll see elks in the town itself. They come in looking for food.'

He found a parking space in the main street and they climbed out into patchy sunshine. 'A quick tour of the centre will stretch our leg muscles, then we'll drive out to see some of the surrounding scenery.'

They wandered along the pavement and—after taking a couple of touristy photographs—she looked at some of the shops but, discovering mainly souvenirs, only went into one, where she bought postcards for friends in England.

Greg was leaning against the car, smiling, when she emerged. 'What have you bought?'

'Three postcards!'

He laughed. 'So you do have some friends back home? Well, what do you think of Jasper?'

'It's much smaller than I was expecting—but, as you say, obviously a meeting-place for youngsters from all over the world. I'm amazed that it hasn't grown much larger.'

'The town has a policy of only allowing home ownership if you actually have a permanent job in the area. It seems to work well. Ready to move on?'

She nodded and asked, 'Where to?'

'I think we'll head for the Maligne Canyon and then on to a couple of lakes. By the time we get there the remaining clouds should have cleared from the mountain-tops.' he climbed behind the wheel and Serina was conscious that he was more carefree then he'd been earlier.

'The canyon is not far and shouldn't be too crowded at this time of year,' he told her with an inviting smile. 'It's one of those places that I remember as much more dramatic when I was younger, but the erosion the water appears to have caused just in my short lifetime makes it less spec-tacular, but fascinating geologically. I expect my increased height has something to do with it as well!'

Delighted by the relaxing effect the Rockies seemed to be having on him, she laughed. 'You could be right.'

'We can walk through the gorge and then get a bite to eat.'

'I'm not hungry.'

He turned and grinned at her. 'You will be when we've finished our hike!'

He was right—she'd never experienced anything like the walk down through the canyon and back again.

When they'd finished their coffee and sandwich he drove on to stop first at a stretch of water surrounded by mountains which, to her amusement, was called Medicine Lake, and then at Maligne Lake. Every time they rounded a corner it seemed that the new vistas surpassed the pre-vious ones and she began to feel that it was too much to properly appreciate such a surfeit of beauty.

As they walked hand in hand beside Maligne Lake she murmured, 'I can certainly see why you feel about the Rockies the way you do. They're incredible!'

He squeezed the hand he was holding. 'And this is just a taster—one day you must see the whole. But that will need at least a week and preferably a month!'

'It won't be this time, then. My ticket obliges me to return when booked.'

'When's that?'

'A week on Monday.'

He looked startled, as if not expecting it to be so soon. 'I thought you were out here for much longer.'

'Nearly three weeks. Long enough when I didn't know Coral and Ed before I arrived.'

'I guess so. Now you know us you can always come back, perhaps with a working visa?'

'Maybe. I wouldn't want to outstay my welcome, though. It was good of Coral to invite me at all.'

'I'm sure Coral doesn't think so. She probably feels she owes *you* something.'

Serina flushed at the compliment. 'We'll see.'

As they walked back to the car Greg checked his watch. 'It's already going on for five, and as it's a clear evening we'll round off the day by taking a trip on the sky tram.'

'Sky tram?'

'A kind of cable-car to the top of Whistlers Mountain. You'll love it. The views are amazing.'

She confided excitedly, 'This'll be a first for me. We don't have many of these back home!'

As Greg purchased the tickets he told her, 'I think you're gonna love the views.'

'I'm sure I am.' The journey, however, was over far too quickly. It was exhilarating and there was just too much to see in the time.

Greg pointed out a distant icefield to her. 'If you get a chance you must take a trip out onto the glacier there.'

The beauty of it all made her tears well up again. Once at the top she begged, 'Can we walk on up to the summit?'

'Not unless you want to walk down the mountain in the dark! I'm sorry, though. The views up there are out of this world.' He smiled and slipped an arm around her waist. 'I'm afraid time's been against us all day. Twelve hours is nowhere near long enough to get even a taste of the area.

'Anyway,' he consoled, 'we're not dressed for it—it's always cold on the walk to the summit and you look frozen already.' He chafed her hands between his to warm them.

She smiled up at him. 'I'm lovely and warm inside.'

His eyes held hers for a long moment and she waited expectantly for his response, but he didn't speak immediately. Instead he tightened his encircling arm and in doing so brushed the swell of her breast, triggering waves of sensation that flooded through her body.

'Unfortunately, if we don't make a move now we'll

miss the last tram down.' His ragged breathing as he spoke told her that he wasn't unaffected by the contact either.

She moved reluctantly. She would have been happy to remain there all night because she knew that the trip down marked the approaching end of their day together, and she hated the thought. When they'd set out she hadn't considered the possibility that, given the slightest chance, her heart would overrule her head.

Despite all the warnings, she felt so at one with both Greg and the mountains that she wanted to believe that he was experiencing a similar empathy. But he gave no sign of it as he strode ahead to the tram station, and she guessed that the day had meant nothing more to him than any other trip to the area.

Dusk was well advanced by the time they climbed back into the cable-car, and the earlier view of the mountains was replaced by a twinkling fairytale valley of lights which sent a tremulous shudder down Serina's spine. Noticing, Greg slid an arm round her shoulders and whispered, 'You'll be back.'

You. Not we, she noticed. She tried to hide the tears which were a mixture of sadness and pleasure. The tram's rapid descent was soon over, and she smiled up at him as they walked round the foot of the mountain.

CHAPTER SEVEN

'I⊤'s the perfect end to a marvellous day, Greg.'

He tightened the arm that was still holding Serina and turned her slightly so that his smiling eyes could hold her gaze. 'We're not finished yet. We'll find ourselves something to eat before we start back to Greenfield.'

'That sounds good.' Wanting to hide the desire that she felt sure must be obvious, she tried to break the eye contact, but when she found it impossible gabbled nervously, 'You know, I still can't believe this place is for real. I thought I was just coming out to Canada for a holiday on a prairie farm.' She waved her free arm around her. 'All this is an incredible extra. I'd heard of the Rockies but didn't realise how accessible they were from Greenfield.'

Clearly amused, he leaned towards her and kissed her— stemming the flow of words. It was something she'd wanted him to do all day and it was everything she'd hoped for, powerful, seductive and yet sweetly gentle. For long dizzying moments she clung to him, responding in a completely abandoned way. He wrapped his arms tightly around her hips, pulling her so close that she couldn't help but recognise that she wasn't the only one aroused.

Sensing that she was rapidly losing control, she attempted to push him away. He grasped her hands and gently trapped them behind her back while his lips continued to search out one erogenous area after another, triggering sensations which until that moment she hadn't known existed.

She could do nothing but surrender to the moment and enjoy the exquisite sensations bombarding the secret parts of her body. When he eventually released his hold on her wrists she somehow found the will-power to free herself from the sweet torture of his lips, but as she tried to move away her knees gave way and he had to catch hold of her again to stop her falling.

99

He held her at arm's length and, searching her face, murmured, 'If only. . .'

Believing that he was trying to find a way to let her know that it had meant nothing at all to him, she snapped, 'There are so many imponderables, Greg. Let's just forget this ever happened.'

When he didn't immediately answer she raised her eyes and was shocked to see the tormented look he was trying to control. 'I'll never forget you, Serina. Never,' he repeated, with an almost trance-like emphasis.

Another trophy for his collection? Was that what he was trying to say? Thank goodness she'd called a halt when she had. It was time he recognised that she was different to all his other conquests. An affair was not and never would be on her agenda, especially when she would be the one left with regrets.

Angrily she freed herself and set off towards the car park without a backward glance.

He followed close behind, and when they reached the car he asked with a wry smile, 'Am I such an ogre?'

She felt her cheeks colour furiously as their eyes met and held. 'I've told you before, I don't believe in holiday romances.'

'And you believe that's what I'm offering?'

When she didn't answer he went on to say, 'Heather's obviously given me a bad press—'

'It's not just Heather. . .' she interrupted sharply, before realising that if she continued with what she'd been going it say it would be obvious to him just how much she did care.

He took her arm and, with a knowing smile, told her firmly, 'Before you jump to too many conclusions I'd like to give my side of the story, but not just at this moment. First we eat.'

He helped her into the car, before driving into Jasper and parking the vehicle at the opposite end of the main street to their earlier visit. Throughout the journey her thoughts were working overtime. Was she wrong about him? He certainly seemed to care what she thought of him, but what possible excuse could he produce that would explain his reputation?

Telling herself to stop clutching at straws and just enjoy the rest of their day together, she climbed from the car and asked brightly, 'Where to now?'

'It's just a short walk to where we're going to eat.'

As they walked to a corner restaurant on the edge of the ribbon development she sensed a tension between them that hadn't been there earlier, and wished that she'd not allowed herself to lose control of her emotions earlier. It had been a wonderful day until then.

The restaurant was busy, but the proprietor obviously recognised Greg and ushered him immediately to a corner table shrouded from the rest of the restaurant by plants.

'Nice place,' she murmured appreciatively, then added hesitantly, 'And not the first time you've been here?'

'It's my regular haunt when I'm visiting this part of the Rockies. They have a way with pasta I can't resist.'

'A healthy way?' she teased, hoping to lighten his mood a little, although she guessed that it wouldn't be easy.

'But of course—what else?'

He waited until the owner had filled their coffee-cups and she'd read through the extensive menu before telling her, 'I'm going for the special on the board.'

She turned to look in the direction he indicated and saw that the special was seafood cannelloni in a basil and tomato sauce.

She hesitated. 'I was going for the salmon, but I must say that sounds a tempting alternative.'

'You won't be disappointed.' As she turned to face him again he raised a quizzical eyebrow and added, 'But don't let me influence you.'

For some unknown reason she was suddenly unsure if he was referring to the food or, more obliquely, to his earlier attempt at seduction, so she told him emphatically, 'I won't, don't you worry!'

He looked surprised by her vehemence. 'So, what's it to be?'

'I'll join you with the special.' She smiled in an attempt to soften her earlier response.

'Would you like any wine or beer with it?'

She shook her head. 'The coffee's going down a treat.'

Until the food arrived they discussed the Rockies, especially the places they'd seen that day. His descriptions of some of the parts she wouldn't have time to visit on this trip made her wish that she wasn't leaving so soon. 'You are really proud of your country, aren't you? Not like the reserved British!'

He smiled sympathetically. 'You must come back and do the full tour.'

'I'd love to one day.'

When the waiter brought the food Serina was amazed by the size of the meal. 'I'll never get through that!' she exclaimed.

He grinned. 'You'll be surprised. There's no hurry.'

Her first mouthful told her that she wasn't going to waste a morsel. 'You were right. I'm certainly *not* disappointed. It's delicious.'

He was clearly pleased that she was enjoying it, and they maintained a companionable silence.

'Coffee?' A waiter was hovering.

'Would you prefer something stronger now?' Greg asked.

She shook her head. 'Coffee's fine.'

He nodded. 'And for me. It's a long drive ahead.'

'I could take a turn.'

He shook his head. 'No way,' he assured her. 'I'm used to driving long distances. This is supposed to be your holiday. You've done more than your share since you arrived in the country.'

Appreciating his consideration, she flashed him a shy smile of thanks before murmuring, 'Before we leave I need to find a loo.'

He pointed her in the right direction and she pushed open the door, happy that their earlier accord appeared to be returning with the food.

A happiness that disappeared when she heard the sound of groaning coming from one of the two cubicles.

She pushed the door tentatively. 'Hello. Are you all right?'

Her question was met by silence. Even the moaning had ceased.

Serina knocked again. 'Are you all right in there?'

This time she thought she could hear the sound of the lock being slowly turned, but when she pushed the door it still offered resistance.

She checked the next cubicle, but discovered that the wall between the two was solid with no gap at either the top or the bottom.

She knew that, if really necessary, it would be possible to turn the lock from the outside but she didn't have anything with her that would do it.

'Please answer me,' she called again.

A stifled moan was the only reply. She opened the outer door and, attracting Greg's attention, beckoned him over.

Frowning, he came slowly. 'What's the problem?'

'I think someone ill may be locked in one of the cubicles, but she won't answer me.'

'Go back in there and try and get her to come out. I'll try and find some tools and, in the meantime, I'll alert the owner's wife in case you need help.'

When Serina reopened the outer door a teenage girl was bending over the washbasin, clutching it tightly.

She rushed over and, putting her arm round the girl, asked, 'Where's the pain?'

The girl gradually unwound herself and turned wide, scared eyes on Serina.

'I'm all right now, thanks.'

The pain must have lessened for she tried to push past, but Serina was too quick for her and took hold of her arm so that she could check the girl's pulse. 'This is no place to bring your baby into the world,' she told her quietly.

Again the girl stared at her, stark fear showing in her eyes. 'How did you know?' she whimpered eventually. 'No one else has guessed.'

Recognising just how young the girl was, Serina told her gently, 'Probably because I'm a nurse.' Noticing the outer door opening slightly, she turned to see a motherly lady peering in with Greg just behind.

'This is a friend of mine—a doctor. He's Greg and I'm Serina. What's *your* name?'

The girl shrank away from her and shook her head. Then as another contraction started she bent over the washbasin again, with Serina gently massaging her back this time.

Greg raised a querying eyebrow at Serina who shrugged. 'Pulse seems OK. I think she's in the early stage. She obviously hasn't told anyone about the baby.'

The moment the contraction began to recede Greg took charge. 'Let's get you somewhere more comfortable before the next one. My car's just outside. If we move now no one will guess what's happening.'

He led the way out and, after looking towards Serina for reassurance, the young girl followed and Serina brought up the rear. She smiled her thanks to the owner's wife and followed Greg and the girl out through the side door.

'Were you with someone in the restaurant?'

The girl shook her head. 'No. No one.'

When they got to the car Serina climbed in the rear seat with the youngster.

'Where are you taking me?'

'To the local hospital.' Greg didn't look at her but kept his eyes on the road.

'I can't—I can't. . .' Huge tears rolled down the girl's cheeks and she wiped them away with her knuckles.

'Tell us your name,' Serina urged.

'Mel,' the girl blurted out.

'Is going to the hospital a problem? Do you know someone who works there?' It was clear that the girl was terrified of someone finding out.

Mel shook her head vehemently. 'I hitched a lift down cos no one knows me here.'

Serina frowned. 'So how did you get into the restaurant toilets?'

The girl looked, if possible, even more frightened and in a voice that wasn't much more than a whisper admitted, 'I know I shouldn't have been there, but I didn't know what to do. I felt so ill.' She wiped away more tears before adding, 'I sneaked through the entrance to the toilet from the garden part of the restaurant.'

Serina nodded and rubbed Mel's back as another contraction racked her tiny frame. 'How old are you?' she asked with a frown.

There was no answer.

'You might as well tell me. They'll have to know at the hospital.'

Mel looked down at the floor. 'Fourteen.'

Greg took out his mobile phone. When it was answered Serina heard him say, 'Dr Andrew, please,' and, after a pause. 'Brad? It's Greg Pardoe. Thank goodness you're on duty. I'm on my way to the hospital with a youngster in early labour. I don't think she's had any prenatal care and there could be problems. Can you organise an ambulance to get her to the city hospital? We should be with you in less than five minutes.'

Brad must have sensed the urgency in Greg's voice as he didn't query the request, and by the time they arrived at the hospital there was an ambulance standing by.

'Stop there.' Greg flung the words over his shoulder as he leapt from the driver's seat. 'I'll just find out where they want us.' He disappeared into the nearest door.

Mel started to shiver, more with fear than anything else, Serina guessed. She put a reassuring arm around the girl. 'You're in good hands now—there's nothing to worry about.'

'I don't want my mum and dad to know.'

'You and the baby are what's important at the moment. Everything else can be sorted out later.'

Greg reappeared. 'Mel, the hospital doctor wants to take a look at you, before sending you off in the ambulance. Just to make sure you'll make it to the city hospital.' He helped the girl from the car and the three of them made their way into a small room just off the main entrance.

Greg beckoned to Serina to leave them to it. 'We'll wait and see what the outcome is, then we must make tracks for home.'

'Will she be all right?' Serina was reluctant to leave the frightened teenager.

'She'll be monitored by trained staff throughout the journey. I suspect she may need a section and, for someone

so young, it's best she's in the city. They're better
equipped.'

He took her hand. 'Cheer up. Brad'll let us know what's
happening just as soon as he can.'

Mel left in the ambulance a very short time later. Serina
wished her good luck, and though Mel momentarily smiled
her acknowledgement she had transferred her trust and
anxieties to her new carers.

Brad joined them. 'Come along to the office for a coffee.
How come you two got involved?'

When they'd explained Serina asked, 'Did you find
anything more about her?'

'No, she's not talking.'

Greg took her hand reassuringly in his. 'A safe delivery
is what's important at the moment. They can discover her
identity when that's sorted out. My guess is that her parents
are out of their minds with worry because she's missing
so it probably won't be difficult to trace them.'

Brad poured the coffee, then asked, 'Have you been up
to see Jean?'

Greg shook his head. 'Not today.' He clearly didn't
want to discuss the matter further as he asked, 'How're
things here? Busy?'

Although she was intrigued by him changing the subject
so obviously, Serina decided that it wouldn't be politic to
ask who Jean was at that moment and so instead tuned in
to what Brad was saying.

'Thank goodness the season's coming to an end. Now,
where are you two staying in Jasper?'

'We're not,' Greg told him. 'I'm on early duty
tomorrow.'

'You don't want to drive all that way tonight,' Brad
exclaimed.

Serina checked her watch and saw that it was nearly
eleven. 'I'd no idea it was so late.'

'Why not stay at my place and leave early? You'll have
a better journey.'

'We can't descend on your wife at this hour.'

'No prob. Erica won't mind.'

Serina was relieved to learn that even if Brad persuaded

them to stay they wouldn't be alone in the house.

'It's tempting,' Greg frowned, 'but it would mean a very early start.'

'Surely that would be better. You both look pretty bushed at the moment.' Without waiting for their agreement, he lifted the receiver. 'Hi, Erica. I've some visitors for you.'

Greg turned to Serina. 'Is that OK?'

She nodded. 'But I'll have to let Coral know I won't be back.'

'When Brad's finished I'll ring Patrick and say I may be a little late in the morning, and he can let Coral know not to wait to up for us.'

'All arranged,' Brad smiled. 'I'll take you over.'

'Could I ring the hospital first?'

'Help yourself.'

Greg rang and spoke to Patrick. Serina only half listened as Brad was asking her about England, but when she heard Greg say, 'I'll ask her and ring back,' she turned to him expectantly.

'Patrick doesn't think there's any point in us returning tomorrow. If we're late he'll have done what's necessary anyway, so he suggests we make a weekend of it. He's checking with Coral if that's OK. What do *you* think?'

There was not a lot she could say, with Brad listening. She'd love to see more of the Rockies. And, if she had to admit it, of Greg. But could she survive three days more alone with him?

'You'd rather not?' he asked with a frown.

'No. I—it sounds fine. I'm afraid I really can't concentrate, though, until I've searched out a loo. I never got to use the last one!'

Brad told her where to find one and she scurried hastily away, relieved to have a few moments to mull over her thoughts. The day's events had left her in no doubt that Greg was attracted to her and appeared to be going out of his way to make her fall in love with him, but she was less sure what he intended to do about it.

If, as she believed, all he was hoping for was a quick affair then she didn't want to know. It wasn't the time

together that was the problem—she knew only too well
that she would enjoy that. She was equally aware, however, that every moment she spent with him would make
her lonely return to England doubly bleak. It had been a
cruel stroke of fate that he had been the first person she
encountered on Albertan soil!

Despite her best efforts, she was unable to think up any
excuse not to extend their stay and she rejoined the men
to find it all settled. Coral had thought it a brilliant idea.

Brad pointed them in the direction of his home and they
were warmly welcomed by his wife, Erica.

She showed them to a twin-bedded room and offered
toilet articles and nightwear, which Serina accepted
gratefully.

When Erica left the room Greg smiled ruefully. 'She
obviously thinks we're more than just friends.'

'And I notice you didn't disabuse her of the idea,' Serina
spat out in a whisper that couldn't be overheard.

'Neither did you!' he hissed, clearly amused.

She glared at him. 'They're your friends.'

He moved towards her, his eyes now glittering angrily
like two chips of coal. 'Exactly. So did you expect me to
complain when Erica had already put herself out for us?
After all, it's not a double bed.'

'I—er—suppose so.' He was right, of course, but it
still left her feeling vulnerable.

Her continuing doubt clearly angered him. 'You really
don't have a very high opinion of me, do you?' He laughed
hollowly. 'I can assure you I have no intention of creeping
into your bed uninvited. I only go where I'm welcome.'

Flushing, she stammered, 'I—er—I didn't mean. . .'
Aware that Heather's jealous remarks were still influenc-
ing her, she sought for the right words to make amends.

Before she could find them he told her gently, 'I think
you did, but I believe I understand why. Now, I suggest
you make use of the bathroom. It's been a long day and
we both need to sleep.'

She crept miserably along the corridor, her thoughts
spinning wildly. What was it he'd wanted to tell her
earlier? Why couldn't he tell her tonight? Was it something

that could make a difference to their relationship, and if so why didn't he tell her now? There was no way she was going to be able to sleep without knowing.

When she returned to the bedroom he was seated on the nearest twin bed, wearing only pyjama trousers.

She smiled wanly and, hoping to encourage him to keep his earlier promise to explain his reluctance to become involved, murmured, 'I shouldn't have said what I did. I guess I'm too tired to see the funny side of it.'

'I did wonder where that English sense of humour was hiding!'

'Thank you, anyway.'

His frown was surprised. 'For what?'

'For a very enjoyable day.'

As she spoke he moved towards her. 'It has been great, hasn't it? And now we have three whole days more to explore my favourite haunts.'

'I'm looking forward to it,' she confessed, depite herself.

Slipping his arms around her, he pulled her close and murmured, 'I take it your earlier dissension was a token protest, then?'

She raised her head to discover his dark eyes watching her with a feral gleam that made her catch her breath. What little will-power she'd had earlier threatened to desert her as he bent his head to find her lips with his own.

'It's me who should be thanking you,' he told her gently, 'because you're a very special person and I've already gone further than I promised myself I would.'

Completely at a loss as to what he was talking about, she turned to him with a frown, but before she could speak he silenced her with a forefinger over her lips.

'Let's just sit down for a moment. I was going to leave explanations until the morning, but. . .' They settled side by side on the edge of the bed, and she had to fight back a giggle at the sudden formality of their position.

'Serina, love. You're my idea of the perfect partner.'

She smiled tentatively as he took her hand and circled her palm with his forefinger. 'But? There's a "but" hiding there somewhcrc, isn't there?'

He appeared to find answering difficult, and when he did so he was unable to meet her eyes. 'I'm afraid there's a very big "but". You've bewitched me, Serina. It would be the perfect end to a perfect day if we could make love, but we can't and you must be wondering why I don't expect it.'

He must have sensed her increasing bewilderment as he drew her towards him then stilled her trembling lower lip with his thumb, before again covering her mouth with his.

'Don't get the wrong idea. I'm a totally red-blooded male who wants to make love to you as much as I believe you want me to.' He smiled down into her eyes as he spoke. 'I've felt that way since I saw you standing so forlornly at the airport, but I've tried to tell myself that I'd get over it. That you were just a passing infatuation I could take or leave, as others have been in the past, but today has proved it's more, much more than that. I've fallen in love with you in a way I didn't think possible—'

'Oh, Greg,' she breathed.

She certainly hadn't expected that and her heart started to pump painfully until he held up his hands to prevent her speaking.

'Before you say anything you'll regret I have to tell you we have no future together.'

'No future?' She winced as she realised that she was parroting him like an idiot. 'Wh-what do you mean?' What on earth was he going to tell her now? That he was married?

'I can never marry,' he told her quietly. 'That's why I've tried so hard to keep emotional involvement at bay. But you've changed all that—'

'Never marry?' she whispered disbelievingly. 'Have you a dragon on *your* shoulder that prevents you responding to the normal need for a wife and family?'

'Not exactly.'

'Not exactly?' There she went again, repeating his words.

'It's not a dragon like yours. You see, I hardly remember my father. He died from a heart attack when I was three.'

'But you missed him?' she probed.

'Not the person—I really can't remember him. What I did miss was a father. And, having seen my mother struggle to bring me up without support in a country that was strange to her, I decided long ago that I wasn't going to expose any woman I loved to a similar risk.'

'But why should you?'

'Dad died of a heart attack when he was thirty-five.'

'So?'

'It's on the cards that the same will soon happen to me.'

'I know that a family history of heart disease is a risk factor, but surely this is going over the top?'

He shook his head. 'I only wish it was. But, you see, his father died around the same age, and I watched a young consultant with a similar medical history do everything in his power to minimise the other risks. He kept fit, watched his diet fanatically, didn't drink, didn't smoke—life wasn't much fun for him. But he still died in his mid-thirties.'

Serina murmured, 'I see, but—'

'That was the day I made my decision not to go over the top, but to live life to the full *and* remain a bachelor. If my dragon's grieving it's for my mortality, not a person.'

'But surely there's so much more that can be done today, even if you are unfortunate enough to suffer an MI.'

'If you're in the right place! But the wide open spaces that mean so much to me also mean that help is usually too far away. The emergency services wouldn't stand a chance.'

The thought of that happening made her want to throw her arms around him and reassure him that she'd stay by him always so that she could save him if it ever happened.

But she knew it was the wrong time. They were both tired and he'd made his decision—perhaps irrationally, and perhaps not. She had no idea what he'd been through as a child.

She couldn't just ignore what he'd been saying, however. 'You were right earlier when you said I wanted you to make love to me,' she told him quietly, 'because I'm already on the way to falling in love with you.' She took a deep breath before continuing. 'However, I'm old-fashioned enough to want it to mean something more than a way of passing the time.'

'Oh, Serina.' He folded her in his arms and, with a heart-rending groan, buried his face in her hair. 'It would never be that, I promise.'

'In that case, I think you underestimate the power of love, Greg Pardoe.'

He lifted his head then and regarded her keenly before groaning, 'I can't take the risk.'

'We all take a risk when we fall in love.' She issued a challenge then. 'I never thought you would be the type not to take a chance on happiness.'

He turned her to look at him, and as he cupped her cheeks with his hands the mute appeal in his eyes tore painfully at her heart.

'Ordinarily, I'm not. But I couldn't be happy taking what I want, knowing that it could be snatched away from us both at any moment and that you would be the one left with nothing more than memories. And I'm convinced that's what will happen.'

She sighed deeply. 'But, Greg. . .' she hesitated, unsure how to phrase what she was trying to say '. . .your reasoning is faulty. You say you love me—if I feel the same way about you and you walk away from me now you'll still make me very unhappy. All I'll have will be memories of one day out together. A lot fewer than I'd have if we'd spent even a short time together.'

'But easier to get over. You're not the type to be alone, Serina. You need to be free to find a partner who'll be with you for life.'

'How can I convince you? One day of happiness with someone I love would be worth a lifetime of marriage to anyone else. And husbands never come with a guarantee, you know!'

'I know you feel that now, but—' He spread his hands in a gesture of despair, then leaned over and kissed her gently on the lips. 'We only met a week ago. There's still time for you to escape without too deep a hurt.'

'You think so?' she queried bitterly, biting back her tears.

'I'm sorry, Serina, to upset you after such a perfect day. I know it's late and not the best of times but I couldn't let you go on any longer, believing that I'm someone who doesn't give a damn whose heart I break.'

She took his hand in hers and, pulling him closer, gave him a kiss that was more sympathetic than sensual. 'I'm glad you have, but I—'

'But you need to sleep on it.' He was clearly determined not to allow her to rush into a decision and she nodded reluctantly, despite an overwhelming desire to wrap comforting arms around him and not let him go.

She slid beneath the covers of her bed, but it was with a painful heart. She'd already learnt that denial of her feelings for him wasn't an easy option. Now aware of just how much he needed love, it was harder than ever and she longed to offer him comfort. She'd originally thought that his reluctance to make a commitment might be down to a bad experience in his past. But this was something she would never have imagined. How could she ever begin to convince him that it didn't matter?

She tossed and turned and heard him doing the same and wished that she had sufficient courage to throw caution to the wind and take him in her arms, but she recognised that if she was ever to change his mind it would have to be done slowly.

When at last she heard the bleep of his wrist watch alarm she didn't feel as if she'd slept for a moment, and made her way to the bathroom in a stupor, unwilling to face him before she'd made an attempt to repair the damage her disturbed night had inflicted.

When she finally emerged from the bathroom Greg was up and Erica had brought them coffee.

'We're welcome to stay as long as we like,' he told her, 'but, if you agree, I'd like to move on and show you Lake Louise, calling on the way at that icefield I pointed out from the sky tram.'

'I think I'd like that,' she told him with a smile.

Over breakfast Erica asked, 'Will you visit Jean today?'

'No,' he replied shortly. 'We're making an early start.'

Serina raised her head, curious to know who they were talking about. The way the name kept cropping up this Jean must be important to him, so why hadn't he mentioned her the night before and why was he now avoiding her look of enquiry? His explanations last night had seemed genuine at the time, but if he hadn't told her about the one person everyone seemed to think he should visit she couldn't help wondering if he was just the finest con man she'd ever met.

She couldn't ask with Erica there, however, but she would certainly do so the moment they were alone.

CHAPTER EIGHT

As THEY started out on their journey, though, Greg was so busy, identifying the various peaks and river valleys they were passing, that Serina didn't have a chance to do so until they reached their first intended stop at the Athabasca Falls.

As they walked towards the noisily tumbling waters she asked, 'Greg? Who is Jean?'

He appeared reluctant to answer at first, and when he eventually did so she found difficulty in hearing his response over the roar of the waters.

'Did you say your grandmother?'

He shook his head. 'She looks after my grandmother,' he mouthed.

Surprised that he hadn't mentioned a relative in the area, she wondered if she was still misunderstanding. 'Where?' she shouted as loud as she could.

'Jasper.'

'Who is Jean?' she asked again.

'A friend,' he answered shortly.

She waited for him to say more. When he didn't she persisted, 'Why did Brad and Erica both think you ought to visit her?'

He turned his head towards her and sighed. 'It's not what I imagine you're thinking. It's— Oh, I can't compete with this roar—let's just enjoy the falls and I'll tell you later.'

Trying to push her curiosity to the back of her mind for the moment, she took several photographs. 'I guess these won't do this spectacular scenery justice,' she murmured. 'I've never seen anything like it before.'

As they walked back to the car he slipped an arm around her waist and told her, 'Jean looks after my grandmother, who has Alzheimer's.'

That had been the last thing she'd expected to hear, and

yet she couldn't help wondering why he hadn't wanted to take her to meet her.

'Do you see much of her?'

'When I can.'

'You should have said, we could have called in today.'

He seemed to have difficulty finding an answer, but eventually he said, 'It wouldn't have been a good idea. She—er—she doesn't usually want to see me and can be quite aggressive at times, so Jean lets me know how she's doing.'

'I'm sorry.'

He shrugged. 'It happens.' He appeared uncomfortable at her questioning, which made her all the more determine to find out the details.

'How badly is your gran affected?'

'She's confused, some days more than others. That's why I didn't want to subject you to a visit.'

Sure now that for some reason he hadn't wanted her to meet this Jean, she told him, 'I think I would have coped. After all, I *am* a nurse.'

Her sarcasm obviously hit home. He touched her hand. 'I understand how it must seem, but it's nothing personal. It's just a pity that Brad and Erica both brought the subject up.'

He paused, searching for the right words. 'It's so difficult to explain.' He sighed heavily. 'You see, I—I never knew her when she was well, or she me.'

Puzzled, Serina asked, 'Why was that?'

'She lived in England and refused to come out here and visit when I was young. She only came out when her sister died and she had no one left in England. I'd started my training by that time.

'Mum did her best, but she couldn't cope for long.' He hesitated. 'You see, she blames Mum—and me—for Dad's early death.'

'But how—?'

'I'm not putting this very well, am I? My father was her son, and Gran's convinced that if it hadn't been for Mum he'd never have left England and so would still be alive. She doesn't accept that his early death is related to that of her own husband.'

Recognising what a difficult time it must have been, she murmured, 'How cruel, after what your mother had been through already.'

He acknowledged her compassion with a half-smile. 'It was. But it's all in the past and I don't intend to burden you with my problems.'

Sad that he didn't feel able to do so, she assured him, 'You haven't. And it helps to share them sometimes, you know.'

He nodded slowly then, shrugging, unlocked the car and told her, 'Back to our tour now. Next stop is the glacier.'

Although she found the incredible scenery fascinating her thoughts continued to stray to what he'd told her. She longed to be the one to show him that he'd been unlucky; that family life could be very different, if only he would take a chance on love. But it was clear that wouldn't happen overnight and the one thing she didn't have on her side was time.

At least now that she knew what she was up against she could do something about it. There must be some way she could convince him that he'd made the wrong decision.

If it had ever been in question she knew now she cared enough about him to try and make him see that he *did* have a future, even if she wasn't a part of it.

He swung the car unexpectedly into a bustling car park and, taking her arm, led her round a chalet-type building and pointed across the road. 'I'll bet you've never seen anything like that before.'

It took a few moments to appreciate that the white landscape opposite was pure ice. 'Why don't those trucks go through?' she asked as a convoy of vehicles carried tourists onto the icefield.

He laughed. 'It's not a frozen lake, it's part of a glacier. Solid ice, nearly a thousand metres thick in parts.'

'Wow. Can *we* take a trip out there?' she asked excitedly.

He nodded. 'You'll need your warm sweater, though. If we had boots we could take a walking tour, but as we didn't expect to be here today a truck tour it'll have to be.'

The trip was fantastic. When they climbed out onto the icefield and the stinging wind lashed their cheeks unmercifully he hugged her close for warmth, and she wished that they could stay there for ever, all problems forgotten.

Once back in the car and on the road again, she looked across at his healthily glowing profile and couldn't believe that in this day and age someone as vibrantly alive as he was could not have a future, but deep down she knew that he was right.

Despite all the modern advances in medicine, young men still died of heart attacks. The thought made her want to draw him to her. To make the most of what time he'd got left. To make up to him for fate's cruel deal.

But even as the thoughts formed in her mind she recognised their futility. He'd long since made up his mind and, as far as he was concerned, that was the end of the matter. He'd closed the file on his life and didn't intend to reopen it, and after all he'd told her she doubted if the short time they had left together would be enough to persuade him to do so.

After a couple more stops to take in the incredible scenery, he told her, 'We're approaching Lake Louise. Is there anything *you'd* like to see or do?'

She sighed deeply and murmured throatily, 'Only convince you that you are making a big mistake.'

He turned his head sharply, before returning his eyes to the road ahead. 'I hear what you're trying to tell me and, you must believe me, I wish like hell things could be different.'

She shrugged. 'They can be, Greg. Believe me.'

They spent two nights in the palatial surroundings of the Chateau Lake Louise, but in single rooms. Greg made sure of that, and Serina wasn't sure if it was for her or his benefit.

They spent an almost idyllic Saturday, walking and driving around the area, and—whilst they did so—chatted non-stop, but every time Serina tried to turn the conversation to his future he changed the subject.

After an evening meal Greg saw her to her room and, as he had done on the Friday, gave her a chaste goodnight kiss. It was as if he couldn't trust himself not to change his mind about his future if he got any closer to her.

As he turned to go she offered tentatively, 'You're welcome to come in—'

He didn't allow her to finish, but shook his head. 'I think it's better if I don't. Then neither of us will get hurt.'

She watched him walk along the corridor with a plummeting heart. If she couldn't make even the slightest dent in his decision whilst they were under the magical influence of the Rockies, what hope did she have?

He couldn't have slept any better than she had for on their return trip on Sunday neither was in a communicative mood.

At her insistence, they called to see his gran.

'I hope you won't regret it,' he told her with a wry smile. 'She can be pretty difficult at times.'

Greg introduced her to Jean, a widow in her late fifties.

'Hi. Good to meet you.'

Not much competition there, Serina told herself with amusement.

'Come and meet Mrs Pardoe,' Jean suggested. 'She's in the front room.'

'Hello, Edna.' Jean pulled Serina forward. 'This is a friend of Greg's.'

'Don't want to see him.' The old lady took Serina's hand in hers. 'You look all right. Not like his mother. She killed my boy—it wasn't his son.'

Frowning, Serina crouched beside Greg's grandmother's chair. 'What wasn't his son?'

The old lady stared at her with blank eyes. 'It'll be teatime soon. Crumpets.' She rested her head back and closed her eyes and, though Serina coaxed her gently, she clearly wasn't going to say anything more.

Jean caught Serina's eye and indicated that they should rejoin Greg, who'd remained in the other room rather than upset his gran. 'At least she didn't tell you to get out of her sight, like she does Greg,'

Serina frowned. 'What did she mean about Greg's mother—?'

'Don't try and make sense of anything she says. She rambles on like that all day. None of it coherent. Now, how about a coffee?'

'Sounds great,' Greg told her, 'and then we must get back on the road. I want to check all's well at the hospital.'

'So, what did you think of her?' he asked when they were back in the car.

Serina shrugged. 'What can I say? It's sad to see someone like that.'

'You were lucky she was civil to you. She never is to me—or Mum.'

Surely he wasn't miffed by her success? 'Isn't that true of most Alzheimer's sufferers? Relatives bear the brunt of their hostility?'

'You're right, of course.' He nodded and flashed her an appreciative smile that warmed her heart.

As they approached the outskirts of Jasper he exclaimed excitedly, 'Look, a bear.'

He brought the car to a sudden halt behind a line of untidily parked cars and she watched the magnificent creature make its way slowly up a grassy slope, away from all the attention.

Serina grabbed her camera and took two quick pictures through the car window. 'That's made my day.'

He leaned across and slid an arm around her shoulder so that he could watch it as well. 'I guess it was coming down to scavenge for food. Didn't think about the sharp-eyed motorists going by.'

When the bear disappeared from view they followed the long procession of cars back onto the road. It was early evening by the time they arrived at Greenfield.

'I wonder if Patrick has had a busy time in our absence?' Greg mused as he drove to the unit.

'It always amazed me how the ward situation could change in just a couple of days off.'

As they climbed from the car he told her, 'You probably won't notice such a great difference over here. There isn't the same concentration of population as you're used to in

England. Consequently, we have fewer emergencies.'

'Wouldn't you prefer to work in a busier hospital?'

'I didn't say we weren't busy.' He stretched his cramped muscles. 'There's plenty to do for the long-stay patients, even if some of my colleagues don't appreciate it.'

'I wasn't suggesting that you had an easy time,' she laughed as they made their way into Reception.

'I'm pleased to hear it.'

While he went in search of Patrick Serina wandered round some of the patients, and was surprised to find Max's old room occupied. 'Is this a new admission?' she asked Sue.

'Yep. He came in early yesterday morning, following a slight stroke. Patrick suggested to Coral that we keep him under observation and carry out a few tests.'

As Serina tried to work out what Coral had been doing at the hospital at that time in the morning Sue opened the door. 'Hiya, Ed. How are you feeling today?'

Serina recoiled with horror as she saw who the new patient was. 'You're the last person I expected to see. What—?'

Unwilling to complete the question she had been going to ask, she shook her head in disbelief. 'Is Coral back at the farm?'

He nodded and his speech slightly slurred, said, 'Where I should be. The harvest—'

'Coral's already arranged for someone to finish the harvesting. I've just spoken to her.' Greg had followed them into the room and, with an encouraging smile, grasped Ed's hand. 'Now all you have to do is to rest and get better.'

Ed shook his head, 'Not here I won't.'

Remembering his dislike of hospitals, Serina turned to Greg and said quietly, 'Couldn't I take care of him at home, like I did Heather?'

Greg nodded. 'Probably. But not immediately. We need to carry out a few tests first.'

'Does Coral need me at the farm so she can visit?'

This time Greg shook his head. 'She and Heather are on their way here already. We'll decide what we're going to do when they arrive.'

Ed watched them closely, then jabbed his chest with his index finger. 'I'll decide.'

Greg grinned and nodded. 'Don't worry. We'll let you have your say.' He flicked quickly through Patrick's case notes on Ed. He winked at Ed then and turned to Sue. 'Keep an eye on him or he'll be out of the front door.'

Ed nodded his agreement. 'Too true.'

Serina followed Greg from the room. 'What happened?'

'Apparently he'd been asleep and got up to go to the loo. He just crashed onto the floor. He was conscious when Coral got to him. She helped him back to bed and kept an eye on him, then brought him in early next morning.'

Patrick came in search of them at that moment. 'Coral's here now.'

She was seated in Greg's office with a cup of coffee, her eyes red-rimmed—whether from exhaustion or tears, Serina wasn't sure. Heather was posed on the edge of Greg's desk, swinging her newly unplastered leg to and fro.

Greg poured a coffee as Coral greeted her. 'Hiya, Serina. I can't believe this has happened. Fine holiday you're having, eh?'

'It's not that bad,' Serina responded with a smile. We've had a great weekend.'

'What did you think of Ed?' Coral asked anxiously.

'He seems OK, apart from a small problem with his speech,' Serina tried to reassure her.

'Maybe, but I don't think he's feeling all that well. I know him better than you do.' Her eyes filled with tears, despite her attempt to put on a brave face. 'I expect he told you that he wants to go home.'

Serina nodded. 'If I can help—'

'That's not the problem,' Coral broke in. 'If he comes homes I know he won't rest. I've hired a contracter to finish off the harvest, but Ed'll be out there, insisting he's doing it all wrong.'

'How long until the harvesting's finished?' Greg asked.

'Another two weeks, I should think.' Coral thought for a moment. 'Though I suppose we could do it in a week if we got two of them working at it. Weather permitting, that is.'

Greg's nod indicated that he was thinking hard. 'Would it be possible to organise that? I can probably spin out the tests for a week—but I don't think Ed would believe me if I try and push it any longer.'

'I'm sure he wouldn't.' She dabbed at her eyes with a tissue. 'I suppose we'd better go and see what he has to say about it.'

'You don't need me, do you?' Serina murmured to Greg as the others left the office. 'Sue looks run off her feet.'

'You're awesome, kid.' He rested his hand appreciatively on her shoulder. 'And to think that in the beginning I suspected you of coming out here to sponge on Coral.'

'You thought what, Greg Pardoe?'

He shrugged disarmingly. 'My mother's fault—she hinted as much.'

'And you believed it?' she muttered furiously. 'Gee, thanks.' She stalked off down the corridor without a backward glance—until she heard him join the others in Ed's room.

He didn't miss her peeking then and winked as he grinned and mouthed the word, 'Sorry', to let her know he'd done it for devilment.

When she'd done all she could to help Serina returned to Greg's office. Coral was there and told Serina, 'After our combined persuasion Ed has agreed to stay put until Greg can arrange the tests, but now he's worried about us women being alone at the farm.'

'There's three of us. We'll be OK.'

'That's what I told him, but the only way to appease him was to agree to Greg joining us whenever he can. Patrick's happy to continue doing the out-of-hours duties so Greg will sleep over at the farm for the next few nights.'

Serina considered it an unwise move. With Heather no longer his patient and the tension between herself and Greg unresolved, she envisaged a difficult few days ahead. 'Surely that's not necessary.'

Coral smiled benevolently at Serina. 'Not exactly necessary, but I thought you'd like the idea.'

Her expression left Serina in no doubt that she'd recognised that there was something between them, and thought she was doing all she could to help their relationship along.

'If it's settled I'll have to go along with it.'

She watched a surprised frown appear on Coral's face and wished she could tell her friend what her problem was, but there was no way she could break Greg's confidence. That was the last thing he would appreciate.

She changed the subject smartly. 'Would you like me to drive Heather back to the farm? We can keep an eye on the harvesting and you can stay here without fretting.'

'I'd certainly like to be with Ed but unfortunately we've only the one car.'

'You could come back with Greg, couldn't you?'

'Of course.' Coral brightened. 'I hadn't thought of that.'

Serina smiled, 'Right. So, where's Heather now?'

'With Greg and Patrick, I think. I'll go and find her.'

Now the fireworks will start, Serina thought. She'll blame me for dragging her away.

She had reckoned without Greg's charm and tact. They walked along the corridor, chatting, and—to Serina's surprise—Heather was smiling.

'Greg says I ought to help Mum by keeping an eye on what's happening at the farm while she stays here with Dad. I don't really want to go alone so would you mind coming back with me?'

'No, of course not.' Impressed by the way Greg had switched the conversation round so that it was Heather's decision to leave, she flashed him a surreptitious smile of gratitude. 'I'm not needed any longer here so we can go at once, if you like.'

'Greg thinks that would be best, don't you?'

Serina watched her unexpected deference with some surprise. Perhaps her father's illness was making her grow up!

Throughout the drive home Heather talked about Greg, and Serina soon realised that the girl's immature crush on the doctor appeared to be subsiding.

'Did you enjoy your trip to Jasper?' Her friendly tone

made it clear that even her previous jealousy at Serina's friendship with Greg had cooled markedly.

'It was great—the Rockies are fantastic, aren't they? I never expected to see anything like them.'

'I hadn't thought about it, but I suppose I was lucky. We spent lots of holidays there when I was a kid. Myself, I've always dreamed of visiting London. I expect you've been there lots, haven't you?'

'Judging by Greg's reaction to London, I think you'd find the crowds there claustrophobic.'

'I know, but I'd love to see the old buildings.'

'I must admit they are spectacular. Perhaps you could come and stay with me for a holiday some time.'

'Could I really? That would be great.' Heather turned the car into the drive of the bungalow. 'Looks like Danny's going ahead well with the harvest. Mum asked me to check that he was happy with everything.'

She parked the car and unlocked the door to the bungalow. 'I'll be back in a moment.'

Serina had made coffee for them both by the time she returned, her eyes shining. 'I'll refill this flask for Danny. Poor lad, it's thisty work.'

Serina grinned to herself as she recognised the reason that Greg was no longer the main attraction.

When Heather returned she downed her own coffee, and almost immediately announced, 'I'll just see if Danny's finishing soon.'

'You could ring him,' Serina told her.

'I'll enjoy the walk.'

Left on her own, Serina settled herself in front of the television. Within minutes she felt her eyes closing. Switching off the television, she stretched out fully and fell into a deep sleep.

She awoke with a start. She could hear both Coral's and Heather's voices. Checking her watch with horror, she saw that it was nearly midnight. She leapt to her feet and rushed out into the kitchen.

Coral smiled a greeting. 'Feel better?'

'I—I—' Serina stuttered. 'I never intended to sleep like that.'

'Don't worry about it. Greg said you've had long day's sightseeing.'

'But I was supposed to be keeping Heather company. I'm so sorry.'

'I would have woken you if I'd needed your help.'

Coral laughed. 'As it was, she seems to have spent the evening entertaining Danny.'

'Mum!' Heather pretended exasperation, but Serina could see that she was well and truly smitten.

She grinned. 'And I haven't even seen him yet! That's why you didn't wake me, is it?'

'I thought you needed the sleep! That's all.' Embarrassed, Heather settled herself at the kitchen table and flicked through a magazine.

'How's Ed?' Serina asked, to change the subject.

'More settled but he'd still rather be home keeping an eye on what's going on.'

'Did Greg bring you?'

Coral nodded. 'He's outside, chatting with Danny to see if he can organise a second driver so that we can complete the harvest in a week.'

'Does Danny have a farm of his own?'

'No. He's a contractor. I know there are more of them, but I'm not sure he'll want to share the work.'

Remembering how Greg had sweet-talked Heather earlier, she murmured, 'I should think that if anyone could persuade him, Greg could.'

'That's why I left them to it.'

Greg came in at that moment. 'All settled. Danny's managed to contact a friend called Scott and he's going to help. He'll be here in the morning.'

Coral nodded her acknowledgement of the arrangement.

'I'm so grateful to you, Greg.'

'Is Danny coming back in?' Heather asked eagerly.

'No. I should think he's probably already left.'

Not best pleased, she muttered, 'In that case, I'm going to bed.'

'Me too, if you two don't object.' Coral gave a huge

yawn. 'It's been a difficult couple of days. Goodnight.'

Wide awake now, Serina started to clear the kitchen. She was placing mugs in the dishwasher when Greg came up behind her and seized her around the waist, before spinning her to face him.

'Fate's not playing fair, is she?' He kissed her again and again, leaving her so breathless that she had to turn her head aside to escape his onslaught.

When she could eventually catch a breath she murmured, 'In what way?'

'To throw us together like this when we went out of our way to be circumspect at the weekend. And just as I was priding myself at controlling my feelings.'

'How can you say that after the way you've just kissed me so thoroughly?' she teased.

'Because,' he told her seriously, tipping her head back with a finger beneath her chin, 'I'm trying to be sensible. I'd love to be with you every moment of the day and night, but it wouldn't be fair to you. Would it?'

When she didn't answer he told her quietly, 'I don't want to hurt you any more than I've done already.'

She half turned towards him and shook her head. 'It's too late for that, Greg.'

He grasped her round the waist and moved closer so that she could lean comfortably against his body. He nuzzled her hair. 'Oh, God, Serina, you're a temptress.'

With a low groan he tipped her chin up again and claimed her lips, tentatively at first then with an increasing urgency as he sensed her growing response.

When his hand slid up to cup the curve of her breast she uttered a throaty moan and snuggled even closer as they sank down onto the nearest chair. His breathing became ragged as his other hand slowly explored the soft mound of her abdomen. When she trapped it between her own hands, he breathed, 'Don't stop me now!'

'Remember we're not alone, Greg. Coral and Heather are probably wondering what we're up to!'

'If they came in at this moment the rosy flush of your cheeks would give us away.' He ran a finger down her face, across her shoulder and down her arm. 'So soft—I've heard of the English rose and now I've met one.'

At that moment a horrendous clanking noise started up outside, sending them both racing to the kitchen window.

'What on earth. . .?' Greg's voice trailed off. 'It looks like the harvesting machine.'

He pulled the door open and rushed out into the night. Serina followed slowly as the noise tailed off and stopped. A muscular giant came forward out of the light of the machine store, wiping his oily hands on a filthy rag. 'Hi. You must be Serina from England. Heather told me about you.'

'You're Danny, are you?' she asked tremulously.

'Yeah. I decided to check over Ed's spare machine now so Scott can make an early start tomorrow if the weather's fine.'

Greg nodded approvingly. 'Is it working OK?'

Danny nodded. 'After a few tweaks.' He eyes missing nothing, he directed a suggestive grin towards them each in turn. 'Sorry to have disturbed your evening.'

'No problem.' Despite being intent on getting away from his gaze as soon as possible, when she reached the safety of the house Serina remembered her manners. 'Would you like a coffee before you leave?' she called.

'No, ta.' Danny shook his head. 'I'm away now. Night, Heather,' he called with a grin, and Serina saw her pyjama-clad figure silhouetted in her bedroom window. 'Sorry if I woke you.'

Greg followed Serina into the kitchen and, hearing Danny's truck depart, he took her in his arms and tried to urge her out of the kitchen, but the spell was broken.

'It's to be another lonesome night, I guess.'

She sensed his disappointment and she had to admit that her own feelings were far from under control, but she tried desperately to ignore them, hoping that if she did so he would think again about the lonely future he'd condemned himself to.

'I think it best if I go to bed now, Greg. Thank you again for a super trip.'

'Will you be able to help out at the unit tomorrow?'

'I shouldn't think so. I guess Coral will want to visit Ed so I ought to stay here.'

He nodded. 'I'll see you tomorrow evening, then. Sweet dreams.' He kissed her lightly, and she made her way forlornly down to her lonely basement room.

When she finally awoke Greg had already left for work.

'I thought you might have gone with him,' she told Coral later. 'Have you heard how Ed is this morning?'

'He's going for scans this morning so Greg said he'd ring and let me know if there's any change in his condition. Otherwise I'll go in when the tests are finished.'

'I want to see how the harvest's going, anyway, so I can give him a first-hand report. I'm just off to have a word with Danny now.'

Serina watched her progress across the yard thoughtfully. Coral had just reached the first field when the telephone rang.

Serina snatched it up before it woke Heather. 'Hiya, honey.' Greg's deep tones made the simple phrase into a caress.

'Oh, hi, Greg. How is Ed this morning?'

'About the same. How are *you* this morning?'

'Fine,' she told him airily. 'Are you busy?'

'Busy enough. Are you able to come in and help us out?'

'No. I'll stay with Heather while Coral visits Ed.'

'That's a pity.'

Serina thought she could hear regret in his voice and, hopeful that he might already be having second thoughts about their relationship, prompted breathlessly, 'Why?'

'I hoped we might be able to do a spot of sight-seeing during the afternoon. Patrick is taking over for a spell at lunchtime.'

Disappointed that it was nothing more, she murmured, 'I'm sorry. Much as I'd like to, I'm needed here.'

'And here,' he countered ruefully, 'but I guess I'm the loser today.'

Heather staggered into the kitchen as he spoke and looked questioningly at Serina.

'It's Greg for your mum, but she's out in the fields. Do you want to speak to him?' Without waiting for a reply, she handed over the receiver—relieved not to have to continue their conversation with Heather listening.

While Heather chatted with Greg she refilled the coffee-machine, wondering if there was enough time for a quick trip to help out at the hospital before Coral needed the car.

'Greg says Mum should go in about eleven,' Heather told her when she'd cut the call. 'Dad's fretting about the crops, so once this morning's tests are completed Greg wants Mum there to stop him worrying.'

Resigning herself to the fact that there was no way she could get to the hospital and back in the time available, Serina smiled and suggested, 'If you want to shower I'll let your mum know the coffee-pot's on and give her the message.'

As Serina was about to leave the bungalow Coral returned. 'Danny's doing a marvellous job out there and so is his friend, Scott, who's helping today and Wednesday and then probably for the remainder of the week. Thank goodness they were both free to help.'

'Are they local?' Serina asked.

'From Greenfield, yes. I expect Heather knew them at school, although they're probably slightly older.'

Having finished her coffee, Coral left for the hospital. Heather drifted back into the kitchen, dressed in jeans and a black T-shirt. 'I'm going to see how Danny's getting on.'

At midday Serina made lunch for them all, but when Heather took hers to eat it with the lads she reflected that she might just as well have gone to the hospital with Coral.

She filled a couple of hours by cleaning the house and preparing an evening meal. Then she locked up and went out to watch the harvesting herself.

Heather was in the cab of one of the machines with Danny and although Serina didn't believe that the cramped cab was the place for the kissing and cuddling that was going on she couldn't see that it was affecting the long swathes the machine was cutting across the field.

'You're behaving like a jealous mother hen,' she rebuked herself, 'looking for some reason to stop their fun.'

Laughing at herself, she decided to go back indoors so

that she was near the telephone. She settled on the settee
with one of the more interesting books on the locality.

She half expected Greg home during the afternoon, as
he'd said that Patrick was taking over, but when the back
door eventually banged open it was already evening and
it was Heather who came in.

CHAPTER NINE

'DANNY'S nearly through for the day so I've come to get a sweater.' Heather rushed through the kitchen, calling over her shoulder, 'I'm going with him. Apparently there's a party in Greenfield tonight so I'll stay over.'

Serina frowned. 'Do you think that's a good idea? Greg told me he was finishing at lunchtime but he's not back yet so we don't know what's happening at the hospital.'

Heather muttered, 'He's probably enjoying himself elsewhere.' She continued hesitantly, 'If—if there was a problem with Dad he would have rung, wouldn't he?'

Sensing Heather's rising anxiety, Serina gave her a reassuring smile. 'I'm sure he would but, just in case it's necessary, why don't you leave a number so that your mum can get in touch?'

'I don't know where the party is yet, but I'll ring her the moment I do.'

'Have a good time, then.'

As Heather was about to leave she turned back to Serina. 'If I let Mum know where the party is you could come with Greg, couldn't you?'

Serina nodded and smiled. 'We could, if Greg's not too tired. Thanks for the thought.'

It was some time later before Coral arrived home, followed shortly afterwards by Greg. Time enough for Serina to wonder where Heather and Danny were partying *and* to worry about her own relationship with Greg.

'All alone?' Coral's eyes were searching fruitlessly for a sign of her daughter.

Serina nodded. 'Heather's gone to Greenfield with Danny. They're hoping to party. She promised to let you know where she is.'

Coral frowned at Greg. 'Have you heard about one tonight?'

'No, but that's not to say there isn't one. We were so

busy all of a sudden, and knowing that I was coming back here, I don't suppose anyone thought to mention it.'

They enjoyed the meal Serina had prepared and then settled in front of the television. Like a regular family, Serina thought ruefully. They were all weary and full of their own thoughts. Coral was worried about Ed and what was going to happen to the farm. They allowed her to talk through, round and over the situation and, though she came to no conclusions, she seemed to eventually relax.

When she closed her eyes Greg and Serina made desultory conversation so that they wouldn't wake her, but even when Serina went out to the kitchen to make coffee Greg didn't follow. She guessed that he must be weary and when she returned with the steaming mugs she searched his face, wishing that she could find a way to relieve just some of the tension and exhaustion evident there.

Coral yawned. 'I'm so tired, I don't think I can wait much longer for Heather to ring. I know her too well. She's probably enjoying herself far too much to remember her promise.'

When Coral left the room Greg raised a questioning eyebrow. 'Alone at last. Ready for bed?'

Deliberately misunderstanding, Serina told him, 'I must say you do look tired. Heather said just before she left that if she let us know where the party was we could join her. I reckon it's a good job she didn't.'

Shaking his head at her response, he crossed the room to sit beside her and—slipping an arm round her shoulder—tipped her chin up so that he could look into her eyes. 'You kept me awake last night,' he murmured accusingly as he leaned across and kissed her.

'I did? *I* slept soundly,' she teased.

'So you didn't have any second thoughts about me?' Determined not to admit that she'd thought of little else, she shook her head emphatically. 'Certainly not.'

'That sure is a pity.' As he plundered her lips again his searching hands moved lightly to outline the curve of her cheek, before slowly blazing a trail down each side of her jaw-bone. When his fingers eventually met beneath her chin her arousal was so great that she unconsciously allowed his tongue to search out the sensitive spots inside her lips.

It was his groan of pleasure as his arms drew her close to his hardening muscles that made her reluctantly push him gently away. 'So, who's having second thoughts now, Greg?'

He brushed her brow with his lips. 'I guess I am. How about you?'

'Depends what you're offering.' She smiled archly. 'You know my reasons for coming out to Alberta—they don't include a casual affair.'

'You drive a hard bargain, love. I wish as much as you that things could be different—'

'I've already told you they can be, Greg.'

'You don't understand.' He rested his head despairingly in his hands.

'I could say the same about you, Greg.'

He shook his head wearily. 'I wish—'

'You wish?'

'I thought you were over here for such a short time that no harm would be done, but I was wrong—so wrong. It's all so hopeless. Much as I want you I know I can't expect—'

'No,' she told him curtly, 'you can't.'

He sighed deeply. 'I don't think this enforced togetherness is good for either of us, Serina.'

'Neither do I,' she told him, frustration making her speak more sharply than she'd intended. 'So, if you didn't sleep last night, the sooner you take yourself off to bed the better.'

He shook his head ruefully and, with another of his chaste goodnight kisses, left her to creep down to her lonely bed.

She was woken by the sound of the combine harvester and shot out of bed to discover Heather, with Coral and Greg, in the kitchen. She must have come back with Danny and her mother was trying to discover what she'd been up to. Heather was not answering her questions, and when Serina made her way into the kitchen the girl seized the opportunity to escape to her bedroom.

Coral clearly was far from happy so when, after breakfast, she left with Greg for the hospital Serina wasn't surprised by her request. 'Keep an eye on Heather, would you? I know you're more or less the same age but I worry about her. You've had so much more experience of life than she has. She's been too isolated out here for her own good.'

Serina raised despairing eyebrows in Greg's direction, but answered, 'I'll do what I can.'

When Heather emerged again around eleven she sank a large mug of coffee, then murmured, 'I think I'll go and see Danny.'

'Did you enjoy the party last night?' Serina asked.

'Uh-huh,' Heather responded noncommitally, before rushing out of the back door to avoid any more questions.

Serina shrugged and settled down to read until lunchtime.

When she'd brewed coffee and prepared a mound of sandwiches she made her way across to tell Heather and the lads that lunch was ready. Heather was up on the only machine working.

Of course, Scott wasn't working again until tomorrow. As the machine came to a stop to see what she wanted Serina sensed a tension between Heather and Danny that hadn't existed the day before. In fact, she wondered if Heather had been crying. However, they elected to continue working whilst eating their lunch so she left them to it, hoping that they would keep their minds on what they were doing. Fooling about on farm machinery could be dangerous.

She'd barely cleared the kitchen and returned to her books before she heard Heather scream and, expecting her worst fears to be confirmed, she rushed to the window.

Instead, she saw what appeared to be the end of a ladder hurtling through the air just across the yard, and as she ran out of the door she heard Heather frantically calling Danny's name and ran towards her.

It wasn't the accident she'd feared that had taken place, so what on earth—?

Her thoughts were shattered in mid-sentence as she saw Danny spreadeagled on the ground, a ladder resting across his legs.

'He climbed up to see how much room was left at the top of the grain store. He couldn't have put it right. It—it slipped. Oh, God, Serina, wh-what can we do?'

One glance at the height of the store told Serina that Danny could be seriously injured. 'Calm down, Heather,' she told the girl quietly. 'Ring the hospital and tell Greg what's happened. Say that I think an ambulance would be a good idea, and then leave everything to him.'

'Are you sure? If Danny doesn't need an ambulance the insurers won't pay.' Her words spilled out in a piping wail.

'In that case, I will,' Serina told her firmly. 'Now do as I say—and calmly. Then bring some blankets back with you.'

Although her voice was calm her thoughts were churning anxiously. Compared to England, they were so far from the hospital and so cut off from help. How long would it take an ambulance to get there? Would she be able to do all that was necessary in the meantime?

Ignoring her fears, she bent down and smiled at the conscious Danny. 'Where does it hurt?'

'I—I'm not sure. All over, I think.'

She counted his pulse and examined his eyes, then slid her hands carefully over his body to check for bleeding.

'Everything seems OK so far. Now, tell me if you can feel me touching you.'

She lightly brushed first his feet and then his hands, and was relieved to discover that he felt every movement. 'Right, I'm going to see if I can lift the ladder.'

She checked the way it was lying and saw that by some miracle it had fallen so that the toe of his boot was taking most of the weight, but she knew that she must move it before it slipped.

Deciding that there was probably no danger of a crush injury as it lay, she carefully—but with a struggle—moved it away.

'Greg wasn't there. Patrick's sent an ambulance,' Heather returned to tell her breathlessly. 'By the way, I asked him not to tell Mum. She'd go spare.'

As it was a warm day Serina covered Danny with only one of the two blankets Heather had brought.

'Shall I make a pillow out of this one?' Heather was already folding it.

'No. Just in case he's done some mischief to his spine, he's best left the way he is until the ambulance arrives with the proper equipment.'

She sat down on the grass beside Danny and between checks on his pulse, she chatted to him.

As the seconds passed she became increasingly anxious. Surely the ambulance would come soon.

'Here it comes,' Heather announced after what seemed like hours to Serina. 'Can I go with him to the hospital?'

'If the ambulance crew says it's OK.'

Serina was relieved to see Greg's car draw up behind the ambulance. He rushed across.

'I thought Patrick said you were in town,' Heather greeted him.

'I walked in as he called the ambulance.' He was already on his knees and examining Danny as Serina had done.

In undertones Serina told him her findings and what she'd done, while he checked Danny's blood pressure with a sphygmomanometer and his eyes with an ophthalmoscope.

He turned to Danny. 'Well, my lad, you don't seem to have done too much mischief.'

Greg nodded towards the paramedics. 'Fit a collar, just in case, then get him to the hospital. Thanks to this little lady, his condition is stable.'

While they did so he rested a hand on Serina's shoulder. 'You've done well,' he told her quietly. 'Certainly kept shock at bay.'

Within minutes the paramedics had applied the collar to stabilise Danny's neck. They then transferred him to a stretcher and carried him carefully across to the ambulance.

'Can I come with you?' Heather hovered uncertainly at the rear of the ambulance.

'We'd certainly appreciate someone.'

'I'll go, please, Serina.'

'If no nursing input is needed that's fine by me.'

The paramedic smiled. 'We'll take her, but you may need to collect her from the hospital later.'

Serina nodded, not bothering to delay them by telling them that Heather's mother was already at the hospital.

As the ambulance set off slowly along the dusty lane Greg repacked his medical bag and Serina bent to pick up the discarded blankets, intending to make her way back to the bungalow. But the moment she moved she started to shiver violently.

While she'd been busy she hadn't thought about the potential seriousness of the situation, but reaction was now setting in. Her legs trembled so violently that she thought they were about to give way and she felt herself buckling at the knees.

Greg dropped his bag again, swept her up into his arms and carried her tenderly indoors. 'I think I'm needed more here than at the hospital. Patrick will easily cope with Danny. Now, what are we going to do with you?'

'I was all right while I was doing something,' she said through chattering teeth. 'It's just thinking of what might have happened. I hadn't a clue what the emergency procedure was over here. Heather was afraid that Danny might have to pay for the ambulance, but I didn't care. I said I'd foot the bill. I hope I did the right thing. I couldn't find any sign of serious injury. I didn't know what else to do.' She knew it was reaction, but didn't seem able to control her tongue. 'We didn't move him, just in case—'

'Whoa. He bent and kissed her lips. 'He's in good hands now. It's you who's important at the moment.'

He settled her down gently on the settee, wrapping her in one of the blankets she was holding before holding her close in an attempt to still the trembling.

'I'm all right, Greg, really. It's just—'

'I know. Thank goodness I was here. Stay there now, and I'll make a cup of tea.'

'Don't leave me.' She clung to him, desperately trying to still her shaking.

He kissed her again and this time she responded eagerly,

deciding that she'd had more than enough of reining in her true instincts. She loved him desperately and she was suddenly convinced that once they'd made love he would change his mind. Hadn't he proved that she already meant something to him by looking after her like this?

'I need you, Greg,' she told him softly. 'I—I want you.' She pulled him down beside her, tears flowing down her cheeks.

He kissed her eyelids lightly. 'But you're forgetting my position.'

She giggled uncontrollably. 'You mean beside me?'

'You hussy!' He kissed her long and hard until her reactive hysteria quietened.

Once sobered, she tried to reassure him. 'I do want you, Greg. Really.' She spoke quietly.

He raised a surprised eyebrow, but didn't speak. Instead he began a sensual exploration of the upper part of her body, slipping his hands beneath her T-shirt to caress her bare skin. When she didn't object he slid her T-shirt over her head, allowing his knowing hands to search out her most sensitive areas.

She felt such a surge of emotion that she was sure there was no going back for either of them and raised her hands to slowly unbutton his shirt. When she'd slipped it off his shoulders she buried her fingers in the mass of soft curls beneath which she could feel his heart thumping wildly.

Savouring the feel and the scent of him, her hands moved slowly over his skin—causing him to groan her name over and over as she ran one hand lightly down his spine.

Pulling her close, he lowered his head until his lips again brushed hers, but as she sought to deepen the kiss he moved slowly away—shaking his head and moaning.

'Greg,' she breathed, 'What—?'

'It's wrong. You don't know what you're saying. It's just the shock speaking—you've told me often enough you don't want a casual affair.'

'It's hardly fair to stop now,' she told him with an agonised moan.

He pulled her tightly against him for a moment, before

moving right away—leaving her feeling rejected and humiliated. 'I'm sorry, Serina, but even if we had a future together the last thing I should be doing is taking advantage of your need at this time.'

Exasperated, she snapped, 'You're not—I've changed my mind—'

'You say that now, love, but when you return to England you'd feel cheated. Believe me, it's best this way.' He kissed her again, before moving away and covering her tenderly with the blanket. 'Anyway, I ought to ring Patrick and see if he's coping.'

'But, Greg, I want you. . .need you. . .'

'Not many of us can have everything we want, love.'

'But surely we can try. . .'

His arms slid around her waist, pulling her close so that he could cradle her head to his chest. 'I'm sorry, love, so very sorry. I should have backed right off the moment I realised how I felt about you but I wanted to make sure you enjoyed your time here.'

'I have, Greg. It's been wonderful and could get better if you weren't so—'

'Serina, love,' he broke in urgently, 'however much you think otherwise, worry about what the future would hold for us would soon sour our relationship—and I couldn't bear that. You're too precious.' He bent and kissed her lightly before releasing his hold. 'Now stay there. I'm going to make that cup of tea.'

Furious with himself for losing control, he made his way through to the kitchen. Waiting for the kettle to boil, he retrieved his bag fom the yard and slammed it angrily into the car, his thoughts black. How could he have been such a fool?

Despite his banter, he'd had no intention of ever allowing things to go this far, but he loved her so much and had so longed to comfort her after the accident that one thing had very nearly led quite naturally to another.

Over the years he'd enjoyed plenty of female company, but always restrained himself from going too far because he knew that he couldn't commit himself. And it hadn't mattered. None of them were important enough to him to cause him great angst. But this time it was different. Serina was special. And now he'd nearly broken his own rules — with the one person he most wanted to protect.

Humiliated by his rejection, Serina slipped on her T-shirt and made her way angrily down to the basement and the safety of her own shower and bedroom.

She was aware of only one thing. He was not going to get away. He needed her love and she would find a way to give it to him, whatever he might think.

When she eventually joined him in the kitchen the tea was poured, and as he handed it to her he kissed her gently.

'Forgive me, darling. Please? Forget this ever happened?'

She shook her head. 'No—I'll never forget.'

He gave her an anguished look. 'You must, my darling.'

'We have so much to give one another, Greg. Can't you see—?'

He nodded before lowering his head despairingly into his hands. 'I know, love, I know exactly how you feel. That's why I've tried so hard not to get too close to you but we seem to be cruelly thrown together time and time again, and I'm only human. I've just broken all the rules I made for myself.'

She raised his head with her hands and kissed him full on the lips. 'You're a fool, Greg Pardoe.'

'I know. But I can't help it. And being alone with you like this is torture.'

After the trauma of the afternoon and his rejection of her, his pig-headed obstinacy exasperated her and she couldn't help herself snapping, 'In that case, you'd better go. Have you rung the hospital?'

Clearly taken aback by her going onto the offensive, he replied, 'I spoke to Coral. She and Heather were just leaving. It seems that your quick thinking probably saved that young lad from any permanent injury. Patrick's going to keep him in overnight for observation but that's all. But I dare say he won't be working for a few days. He'll ache all over tomorrow.'

'That's—'

She was about to express her relief when he interrupted

her. 'By the way, with all the excitement I almost forgot my news. I spoke to Brad this morning. Mel had a little boy. Poor kid had a prolonged labour but is fine now, and you'll be pleased to know there *is* a happy ending. Her father and mother have been traced and are delighted with the baby. Seems they always wanted a boy but never managed it.'

The good news went some way to calm her irritability and she exclaimed, 'That's wonderful, Greg. If only *we* could be sure of such a happy ending.'

An ironic lift of his eyebrows left her in no doubt that he considered that an impossibility. 'Miracles are few and far between.'

'But—'

'You're still searching for the fairy-tale ending?' He wrapped his arms around her and hugged her to him.

'I wish desperately it was within my power to grant you even the smallest miracle.'

Disentangling herself, she sighed deeply. 'You *might* be the exception,' she told him. 'It's silly to give up hope. . .' She lifted her head, her eyes beseeching him to agree.

'My darling, hope's the one thing I don't have. Love by the bucketful, but. . .'

'But you're not prepared to share it.' Tears of frustration spilled down her cheeks. Holding her face gently between his enormous hands, he wiped away the tears with his thumbs. 'You're so beautiful, Serina. Don't waste your life on a no-hoper.' The anguish in his voice told her that it wasn't self-pity speaking. He really thought what he was doing was right.

'But, Greg, I—'

'Don't say it, Serina. My emotions can't take much more!'

Sure that he was putting the blame for that on her wanton behaviour, she told him firmly, 'No, Greg. I'm going to have my say. For the first time you've shown me how you really feel. Nothing else matters—'

'How can you say that?'

'Quite easily, and so can you if you put your mind to

it. You say that you don't want me struggling to bring up a family if anything happens to you. So? We just won't have a family. I wouldn't mind as long as I have you.'

'You say that now, but it's not that easy. You would probably come to hate me for trapping you in a childless marriage and that would be, well, unbearable.'

He pulled her into close contact with his body. 'You mean too much to me.'

'Oh, Greg, you've got it so very wrong.' She was so overcome by the desire flowing between them that she couldn't continue. With an effort she tore herself from his arms, the tears streaming down her face. 'If you're going to go I suggest you do so now because your inconsistent behaviour is doing absolutely nothing for my emotions either.'

'Is yours any better?' he queried, attempting to take hold of her again, but she'd had enough. 'Go, for heaven's sake.'

As he strode angrily out of the bungalow she felt too weak to move, but willed him to have a change of heart and come back.

When he didn't and she heard his car leave she went down to her bedroom and threw herself onto the bed in a paroxysm of self-loathing, wishing that she hadn't behaved so stupidly. What must he think of her now? She'd told him often enough that she didn't want an affair and she'd meant it—until that afternoon.

When she eventually felt able to face Coral and Heather she was relieved that neither appeared concerned at her absence when they had arrived home.

They were both far too worried about their own problems. Coral was agitated about the accident, worried if insurance would cover any claims and even more worried about the harvest.

'I just hope Scott comes again tomorrow,' she told them not once but once every half hour. Heather barely spoke all evening.

When she felt she could reassure Coral no more Serina took herself off to bed with the excuse that she'd had more than enough excitement for one day. She knew that Greg

returned later from the hospital, but she had no intention
of facing him again that day. She'd made too much of a
fool of herself to do that.

Coral woke her with a cup of tea the next morning when
she and Greg were about to leave for the hospital in
convoy.

'You should have woken me earlier. It's so dark and
quiet down here in the basement that I just sleep on.'

'I expect it's doing you good. I'm sorry to disturb you
now, but I wanted to let you know we were leaving. Scott's
working out in the field and I've left Heather still asleep.
She did talk about going back to work this week, but she's
obviously not ready yet.'

When Heather eventually joined her much, much later
in the morning she was white-faced and glowering.

'Everything all right?' Serina asked cheerfully.

She was answered by an even blacker look, but not a
single word until she started to prepare sandwiches
for lunch.

'Serina?'

'Yes?'

'Can I talk to you?'

'You are doing so already.' After being ignored all
morning, she didn't intend to turn and look at the girl
immediately so she was startled to hear her sobbing.

Quickly rinsing and drying her hands, she put an arm
round Heather. 'What on earth's the matter?'

'I—I don't know what to do.'

'About what?'

She swallowed hard. 'I let Danny make love to me on
Monday night and I don't want to be pregnant like that
girl Mum told me you found in Jasper.'

'You're not on the Pill?'

Heather shook her head.

'And Danny. Did he use anything?'

She shook her head again. 'I don't think so. I'd drunk
too much or I'd never have let him. And when I tried to
talk to him about it yesterday he didn't want to know—he
said there was nothing to get worked up about. I shouted

at him, told him I wished he was dead and then he fell
off the ladder.' Tears flowed down her cheek. 'So, you
see, the accident was all my fault as well.'

'Of course it wasn't. He should have been more careful
about positioning it. Anyway, he's going on all right. It's
you I'm worried about at the moment. Now, can you tell
me when your next period's due?'

'No. They don't follow any pattern.'

Serina sighed but, after questioning her further, decided
that Heather probably did need the morning-after pill. But
how to go about getting it prescribed in Canada, she had
no idea. And, when asked, neither did Heather.

Serina thought fast. 'Coral said she'd come back after
lunch. You and I will go the hospital then, saying we're
going to visit your dad and Danny, and I'll sort something
out for you somehow.'

'You promise?'

'I promise.'

They were ready to leave the moment Coral walked
through the door. 'Heather can't wait to see how Danny
is,' Serina told her by way of explanation.

When they arrived at the unit she said to Heather, 'You
go and see your dad and I'll see what I can do.'

Aware that Heather had put her in an impossible position
after the events of the previous afternoon, she tapped nervously on Greg's office door. When there was no answer
she opened it a slit and saw that he was tidying away the
papers from his desk.

'I need to talk to you, Greg.'

He looked up, a sheaf of papers in his hand. 'Hiya.
Can't it wait?' he queried, a touch of impatience in his
voice which suggested that he wasn't pleased to see her.

'I need your advice. It shouldn't take long.'

He looked up at her expectantly as she closed the door
behind her.

'I want to talk to you as a doctor, Greg, and not as a
friend. In total confidence. I don't know enough about
your health service to deal with this on my own.'

'About the accident?' He sat back onto the chair behind the desk.

Serina   shook   her   head.   'No.   About   the morning-after pill.'

'What? Why? We didn't—'

'It's not for me,' she interrupted quietly. 'It's for Heather.'

He looked at her, aghast. 'Heather? You say, Heather?'

'Yes. There was no party Monday night. She spent the night with Danny. She doesn't seem to know whether he took precautions, and he wouldn't tell her.'

Greg raised a hand to his head. 'Has she never heard of—?'

'AIDS?' Serina filled in for him. 'Or other disease?' She shrugged ruefully. 'Of course she has. But she'd been drinking and didn't think.'

Greg gave a despairing groan. 'Stupid—stupid girl.'

'What's done is done, Greg, and I'm sure Heather won't make the same mistake again.'

He raised his eyes to the heavens. 'What a mess. And just when I have to get to Jasper as soon as possible.'

'All I need to know is the way to go about it. I'm not asking you to prescribe it.' As his earlier words penetrated her own worries she asked, 'Why do you have to go?'

'My grandmother's playing up. She's decided she wants to go back to England, but she's got no one at all back there. I'll have to try and reason with her.'

'I thought you said she doesn't usually want to see you.'

'There's no one else, and I am her only blood relative.'

'What about your mother?'

'It's not her problem. I wish it wasn't mine, but—'

'Would you like me to come with you? She seemed happy to talk to me the other day.' She made the offer instinctively because she recognised the difficulties ahead of him.

'No.' He told her bluntly. 'You're needed at the farm.'

He must have recognised her surprise at his curt refusal for he softened his tone as he added, 'Anyway, I can't leave immediately. I must sort out Heather's problem first.

I'm sure a few minutes either way won't make any difference.'

'Don't be too hard on her, will you? I think she's already learnt her lesson.'

'Yes, ma'am.' Watching her with a penetrating intensity, he touched an imaginary forelock and murmured, 'I suppose I was almost as guilty. I took advantage of your distress following the accident. *And* after I'd promised myself I'd do nothing to hurt you.'

'That's what I thought when Heather told me. ''There but for the Grace of God. . .'''

He groaned and, pulling her close, kissed her gently. 'I'm so sorry, love, really sorry. All I succeed in doing is making you unhappy.'

When she could free her lips to speak she murmured, 'I'm not complaining, Greg. Just remember that.'

'Oh, Serina, love, I don't deserve you.' His cry was anguished and she longed to find a way to make him accept her love. But there wasn't time. There never was, it seemed. This time he had to see Heather and then make for Jasper.

'When you return I'll show you what you've done for me. How you've chased my dragon away.'

He shook his head. 'I'm delighted if I've managed to tame your dragon, love, but the last thing you need is for me to leave you with another one for company. And that's what's going to happen if we're not careful. That's why the best thing would be for us not to be alone together—'

'No—' Unable to believe what she was hearing, Serina began to protest.

As if he hadn't heard he broke in, 'It's not that easy, though, is it? Especially when you're living at the farm and helping out here. When I get back I'll suggest to Coral that you have a proper holiday and perhaps make other arrangements for security at the bungalow. Anyway, it's time I did some out-of-hours duties at the hospital.' He kissed her again, a long and lingering kiss, then— muttering that he must find Heather—he rushed from the room.

Stunned by what he'd said, she made her way down to

the car park. With only her thoughts for company, she settled in the driving seat of the car and waited for Heather.

She couldn't see what more she could do. She'd tried to prove to him that nothing was impossible where there was love. Even if she'd failed she would never have forgiven herself if she hadn't tried.

CHAPTER TEN

AFTER what seemed like hours, but Serina's watch told her was much less, Heather found her.

'This is where you're hiding, is it? I'd begun to think you'd left without me.'

Serina managed a weak smile. 'I would have been in Greg's way had I stayed in his office. He was trying to tidy away his papers, before leaving for Jasper.'

'He's just going now—see.' They both waved as he drove out of the car park. 'I came to thank you. . .' she seated herself beside Serina '. . .for being so kind. Greg was wonderful and we've sorted everything out.'

'He gave you the pills?'

'No. Funnily enough, Nature took a hand. I don't need them after all.'

'You mean. . .?' Serina frowned and then, remembering the girl's irregular cycle, spared her further embarrassment by saying, 'I see.'

'Greg said if I was going to do something so irresponsible at least I did it at the right time. If you get my meaning.'

Serina nodded, intending to change the subject, but Heather continued, 'Greg was still worried about the risk of disease so he went to see Danny. He wouldn't tell me what they talked about, but after their chat he seemed happy that I was at no risk.' She hesitated. 'You won't tell Mum, will you, though? I promise this is the last time I'll do anything so stupid.'

'We all have moments of madness in our lives. I know I have. I suppose it's the only way we learn.'

Recalling her own moment of madness the day before, she sighed. Realising that she was becoming quite fond of Heather, she slipped an arm round the girl's shoulders. 'Let's forget any of this ever happened, shall we?'

Heather nodded. 'That'd be best. Mum's not a fan of

the contraceptive pill, as it is. If she knew what I'd been intending she'd have blown her top. Thanks for being so understanding, Serina.'

'As I said, we're none of us perfect and—from what I've seen of her—your mother would be the first to understand.'

Heather nodded sulkily. 'She's not your mother, though, is she?'

'That's true.'

Her expression must have given her sudden feeling of sadness away, as the girl clasped her hands to her mouth. 'Oh, I'm sorry, Serina. I've put my big foot in it again, haven't I?'

'Not at all,' Serina reassured her. 'I asked for it by poking my nose where it wasn't wanted.'

Heather laughed. 'It's difficult to remember you're only a couple of years older than me—I suppose your training as a nurse gives you that air of authority.'

Serina smiled. 'Now you're making me feel ancient. Come on, let's go and see your dad for a few minutes and then get back to the farm.'

They found Ed, fretting. 'What's happening to the harvest, Heather? Has your mother found anyone else?'

'Danny's friend, Scott, is carrying on. It'll just take longer with one.'

'The sooner I can get back to it the better.'

Serina rested a hand over his. 'It's going well. Let Greg finish his tests and by that time you should be in better shape and will be more use. If you start trying to do too much too soon you'll be back in here for even longer.'

'I know that, but if I was on the spot I could make sure it's being done right.'

Serina winked at Heather. 'Do you think he would rest indoors?'

Heather shook her head and grinned. 'Never. He'd be straight out into the fields.'

'In that case, I think you're better off here. Resting. And, that being the case, we're going to leave you in peace.' She turned to Heather. 'I'm going back to the farm now. Are you coming or staying?'

Heather shook her head. 'If you don't mind, Dad, I'll pop along and see Danny. I expect Mum'll be in later. I'll get a lift back with her.'

'Give him my best,' her father told her. 'Tell him I was sorry to hear what happened and hope he's feeling better.'

'He is. I think he'll be going home tomorrow.'

Serina left the room behind Heather. 'He looks tired, doesn't he? Probably best if we leave him to sleep.'

Heather nodded. 'I'll see you later, then.'

Serina drove thoughtfully back to the farm, wondering what was happening in Jasper and whether Greg had sorted out his grandmother's problem.

After a cup of tea together Coral returned to the hospital and left Serina with little to think about but Greg. She tried to watch the harvesting from the bungalow windows, but Scott was out of sight and she didn't want to leave the telephone. However, it rang only once and then it wasn't Greg. It was an enquiry from Heather's office that Serina couldn't answer.

She flicked from channel to channel on the television. Anything to fill the time. She was far too restless to read. Thoughts of Greg were playing havoc with her emotions.

It was a relief when she saw Coral's car, coming down the lane, even though she knew it was a forlorn hope to expect Greg to be with her.

'How's things?' Coral greeted her.

'Fine. Just a message for Heather.' She handed the young girl the scribbled note.

'Greg rang,' Coral told her as she took off her coat.

'How—how's it going?'

'I think he's winning so he's staying in Jasper. He wanted to let me know he wouldn't be back at the bungalow tonight.'

Serina's heart plummeted with dismay. Was she so unimportant to him that he didn't consider her worth a personal call?

After what he'd said earlier she supposed that she was. Heather knew him better than she did and had tried to warn her, but she had been arrogant enough to think that she could change him.

Shame flared in her cheeks at the thought of her behaviour the day before. Why, she'd almost thrown herself at him. When the conversation returned to Greg she was surprised to hear Coral say, 'Poor Greg, he's in an impossible position.'

'Why's that?'

'His mother refuses to become involved with his grandmother's problems again, and there's no way he can keep an eye on her while he's working. But he feels responsible. That's why he pays for her to be looked after and why he has to be the one who sorts it out.'

'I didn't realise—'

'Even though he hardly knew her, he found the best home for her he could but she didn't settle. I don't know what he'd have done if Jean hadn't been willing to take her into her own home. And if she refuses to stay there goodness knows where else she can go.'

'How did he find Jean?'

'Brad's wife told Greg about her.'

As soon as they'd finished eating Serina made an excuse to take herself off to bed so that she could digest this new information about him.

He was such an enigma. In the beginning she had thought him self-centred and inconsiderate, but the more she learnt about him the more it seemed she'd been wrong. If anything, he cared too much about other people. Otherwise he'd never have come to the decision he had to deny himself the thing he needed most of all—someone to love. If only she hadn't behaved so badly the day before they could at least have remained friends. It was no wonder he hadn't rung her.

She couldn't sleep. At least, not until the early hours of the morning. Consequently it was late again when she was woken by Heather, shaking her gently and whispering, 'Serina, do wake up. Greg wants to speak to you.'

'What? Where?' Unable to focus immediately on what Heather was saying, she grasped the mobile handset that was thrust into her hand and mumbled, 'Hi.'

'Sorry I didn't get back to you last night,' Greg's deep brown voice greeted her. 'I was going to ring you after

I'd contacted the hospital but Gran woke, and by the time she was settled it was too late to disturb you. I guessed Coral would tell you that I wouldn't be home.'

Of course. He had to let the hospital know if he wasn't going to be back for his morning shift. She should have realised that instead of torturing herself as to why he'd rung Coral but not her.

'How is she now?' she asked.

'Confused. But the funny thing is that for once, she actually seemed pleased to see me. Which meant that, after a lot of talking, I was able to persuade her to stay where she is for the time being. So I feel able to make my way back to Greenfield.'

'It must have been difficult for you, Greg.' She wanted to say more, so much more—to let him know that she understood. Instead, she asked, 'When do you expect to get back?'

'I should be back at work within a couple of hours. At the moment I've stopped for a coffee. I just wondered if you are going to help out at the unit this afternoon?'

'I—I'm not sure. I'll have to check with Coral what's happening.'

'Do try, Serina,' he urged softly. 'I missed seeing you last night.'

Not a little put out by his contrary behaviour, she retorted, 'You'll have to get used to me not being there every night from Monday. I'll be back in England.'

'Don't remind me. I can't believe your holiday is nearly over.'

The regret in his voice gave her an unexpected feeling of satisfaction. Perhaps she oughtn't to be quite so accessible.

He was speaking again and she dismissed her own thoughts in time to hear him say, 'Come over, if you can. There's so much to be done at the unit. See you.'

She was thoughtful as she took the telephone handset back up to the kitchen. She couldn't deny that she'd love to see him again, especially when she had so little time left in the country, but would it be wise?

After a quick shower she went out into the fields in search of Coral and Heather. 'I expect you heard Greg's on his way back?' When Coral nodded she continued, 'What are your plans today?'

'I've promised Ed I'll stay home and keep an eye on what's happening here so I won't be going in until this evening.'

'In that case, could I use the car and go and help for a little while?'

'If you really want to. You know my feelings. I invited you out here for a break, and you certainly haven't had one as yet. However, if you insist on going in you could go with Heather. She wants to see Danny and—if he's discharged—take him home.'

'They've become very close, very quickly, haven't they?'

Coral nodded. 'I don't mind. I know his family. He's a good lad and works hard and is more of an age with her than Greg.'

Serina wondered what she would say if she knew what had taken place on Monday night but it wasn't her place to tell, especially as she was sure that the events that had followed had made such a lasting impression on Heather that she would consider her future actions much more carefully.

Heather came through from her bedroom. 'Right, I'm ready. See you later, Mum.'

'Serina's coming with you—to see if she can help. She's a glutton for punishment.'

Guessing that both Heather and her mother believed that seeing Greg again was probably more of an attraction than the work, she muttered, 'Not really.' To hide the colour she knew was flaring in her cheeks, she turned and fled down to the basement. 'Won't be a moment,' she called over her shoulder. 'I'll just collect a sweater.'

'What can I do?' she asked Kathy on their arrival at the unit.

'If you don't object, it'll be baths and bed-making again. It's such a help to get those done before lunch.'

'That's fine. It gives me a chance to chat with the residents as we move around the unit.'

'We've got a new chappie you might find willing to share his early memories. He's next door to Ed. Only came in yesterday and hasn't spoken much so far. His name's unpronounceable but apparently he's always been known as Abe.

'Wanda's already started the round. She'll be about halfway down the first pod.'

'I'll find her.' As she spoke Serina was already on her way out of the office.

When she caught up with her Wanda welcomed her warmly. 'Gee, Serina, this is great—am I glad to see you.'

They worked well together, and as lunchtime approached they reached the new patient's room—the last on Wanda's list. Serina tapped on the door and saw Abe sitting by the window, gazing at the fields that spread into the distance without interruption.

'Hi, Abe. Shall we make up your bed for you?'

'Done it,' he told them proudly.

Serina looked round 'You've done it pretty well—in fact, it's exactly as we would do it. Are you sure you went to bed last night?' she teased.

'My wife was a nurse. She taught me. I don't need no help.'

'We can see that. Anything else we can do for you while we're here?' Serina recognised the loneliness he was trying to hide and sought to engage him in conversation.

He shook his head sadly. 'Only turn back the years.'

'I wish it were possible—for all of us,' Serina smiled, 'but, as we can't, if you'd like to talk about old times I'd love to hear about them.'

'You've all too much to do.'

She shook her head. 'Not me. I'm a volunteer and don't have any specific duties. In fact, my time's my own from now on.'

Wanda smiled and left the room, and Serina pulled up a chair beside the obviously uncertain Abe.

He remained silent, and she didn't speak immediately but took one of his hands between hers as he wiped away silent tears with the other.

When she considered that he had regained control she urged, 'Tell me about it.'

'I miss the wife. We did everything together.' He sniffed unhappily, trying to regain control. 'I'm sorry to be such an old fool.'

'You're not,' Serina assured him. 'If you didn't miss her I would be more surprised. When did she die?'

'March—I was just in the way then. Our son, Al, took over the farm some time back. Once I was on my own Al's wife persuaded him I'd be better off here with people I knew. She couldn't stand me crying, see.'

Serina remained silent while he wiped away another trickle of tears. 'It must be hard to leave the place you've known all your life and move in here, even if you do know some of the other residents.'

'Only one or two and then not well. We kept ourselves to ourselves, did me and the wife—we didn't need anybody else.'

She nodded. 'Perhaps you'd enjoy meeting up with some of the others now and again.'

When he didn't answer she murmured, 'I can imagine how lost you must feel at the moment. Change is never easy, but it's something we all have to go through—often when we're least expecting it.'

He rested his free hand on hers and shook his head. 'I thought you too young to know, but you've been through something similar, I guess.'

Serina nodded. 'You're right but, as you can see, I've survived and although I'm only over here on holiday for a short time I'd love to hear something about your early days on the farm.'

He turned to her then, tears streaming down his cheeks. 'You really mean it, don't you? You really want to hear what I have to say. Not like Al.' The thought of his unreceptive family dried his tears.

Serina nodded. 'I certainly do. And, I can tell you, when you get to know everybody a little better I think you'll enjoy it here. Most of the others seem to.' As she spoke she heard the door open, and turned to see Greg and Patrick coming in.

'Sorry to interrupt, Abe.' Patrick moved over quietly to sit on the bed. 'I brought the regular doc along to meet you. This is Dr Pardoe, known locally as Greg.'

'Hiya.' Greg shook Abe's hand. 'I see you've found a friend already.' He nodded approvingly in Serina's direction. 'But, be warned,' he teased, 'she'll give you no peace until she's discovered every detail of your past.'

For the first time Serina saw Abe smile. 'I'll watch her, don't you worry. It'll be a pleasure.'

'I'll leave you with her for the moment and be back to see you later.' As he spoke he squeezed Serina's shoulder reassuringly, before winking imperceptibly and turning on his heels.

Before she had a chance to respond he was gone.

'Seems like a nice guy,' Abe ventured. 'Now, where would you like me to start? When we bought our first quarter of land in Alberta?'

'Sounds a good idea,' Serina encouraged.

For the next hour, until they were called for lunch, he described his early days so vividly that Serina couldn't make notes fast enough.

After settling Abe at a corner table in the dining area and introducing him to Ed, she wandered off to find Kathy and see if her help was needed elsewhere.

'Coming for a bite of lunch, Serina?' she heard Greg call from somewhere behind her.

She turned to see him coming from one of the rooms. 'If Kathy doesn't need me for anything.'

Kathy came out of the office at that moment. 'No. You two go on down.'

Picking a crisp salad, Serina settled at an empty table while Greg ordered his choice from the pasta menu and poured out two glasses of water.

He grinned at her as he took his seat. 'Well, you certainly worked wonders with Abe. Patrick was worried about him. Said he was withrawn, and refusing to talk to anyone. Then I come in and find him a picture of animation. How on earth do you manage it?'

Feeling a warm glow at his approbation, she smiled. 'He reminds me of Max. He needs someone to talk to and

I wanted to hear what he has to say. It was easy. But he does appear to have severe angina. I know he was excited, but I felt the number of pills he was popping under his tongue a bit excessive.'

Greg frowned. 'Glyceryl trinitrate?'

She shrugged. 'I guess so. He took three of them during our conversation.'

'Any skin-flushing?'

'Difficult to tell. His outdoor life has left him with a ruddy complexion, but he certainly complained of a head-ache as I walked him through to the dining-room.'

'Hmm. That could be the tablets or it could be due to him being anaemic, as Patrick suspects.' He was obviously puzzled. 'There's nothing in his notes about angina, and Abe obviously didn't mention the tablets to Patrick. After lunch I'd better try and get the result of the blood test that was done earlier, and then have a chat with him. Sounds like he needs sorting out.'

'If he has severe anaemia couldn't that be the cause of chest pain?'

'It certainly could.' Greg looked impressed by her knowledge. 'In which case it needs to be treated very differently, as you obviously know.'

Experiencing a warm surge of pleasure at him including her in his assessment of Abe's health, she murmured, 'I guess so.'

'I need to see him sooner rather than later. Perhaps you'd come along with me after lunch.'

She nodded, before asking about his trip to Jasper. 'You think she'll stay where she is?'

'For the time being. I expect it'll happen again, though. I was lucky to get through to her when I arrived because this morning she was as cussed as ever.' He grinned. 'Must be where I get it from.' He pushed back his chair. 'Finished? Let's go and find Abe, then.'

She sat quietly while Greg documented Abe's medical history, but she was as puzzled as Greg when he didn't mention a heart problem.

Eventually Greg queried, 'Has a doctor ever suggested that you might have something wrong with your heart?'

She smiled encouragingly, and when Abe slowly shook his head she said quietly, 'What about the pills you were taking earlier? Who gave you those?'

He shrugged. 'Those? The doctor didn't give them to me. They were the wife's. I had the same sort of pain so I thought they might help.'

'Could I see them?'

Greg took the pack from him and nodded towards Serina. 'Glyceryl trinitrate. Did they? Help, I mean?' he asked Abe.

'Sometimes, not usually. I found them in my pocket this morning so I thought I'd give them another try.'

Greg nodded. 'I'm not surprised they didn't do the trick. The other doctor did a blood test this morning and I've got the results here.'

'It's a bit thin, is it?'

Amused by his description, Greg agreed. 'It is that. We're going to have to pump you full of iron.' He laughed. 'I was going to say, put some colour in your cheeks—but you don't need it there, do you?'

'No. The sun and the wind have seen to that.'

'I'd like to keep hold of these tablets for the time being and initiate some tests to see if you really need them. If you get the pain in the meantime tell us immediately and we'll give you something.'

Abe nodded. 'I haven't been right since the wife died. I suppose I just hoped her tablets would do the trick.'

'When we've sorted your blood out I think you'll feel a different person. You'll have so much energy you'll be chasing us all up and down the corridors.'

'I certainly don't feel like it at the moment.'

'Can I just take a look at you?' Greg asked.

Serina took Abe's jacket and shirt, then helped him up onto the bed.

Greg carried out a thorough examination, checking Abe's chest especially intently.

Eventually he removed his stethoscope and grinned. 'I really can't find much wrong there, but we will need to do a few tests before we can say definitely.'

Abe seemed pleased. 'Thanks, Doc.'

'I'll be back to hear more of your early struggles later today or tomorrow,' Serina assured him as they left the room.

'What a delightful man,' Greg said as he closed the door of Abe's room. 'What are you doing now?'

'I ought to see if I'm needed elsewhere and I must find out when Heather is leaving, otherwise I could be stranded here.'

He laughed. 'You're too late. She left with Danny before lunch.'

'She might have told me. What do I do now?'

'You have several options,' Greg told her, ushering her into his office and closing the door.

'Such as?' Serina was somewhat miffed that Heather hadn't bothered to tell her she was going.

He poured them both a coffee before answering. 'Take my car, wait for Coral to visit Ed this evening or, best of all, stay with me.' As he finished speaking his arm encircled her waist and pulled her close. 'What do you say?' he murmured, lowering his lips firmly onto hers, thus preventing any reply.

Remembering her earlier decision not to be so readily available, she struggled to free herself. 'I'll wait for Coral. That'll give me a chance to chat with Abe again.'

She saw the disappointment in his eyes. 'That'll mean a long shift for you.'

Without answering, she picked up her mug of coffee and seated herself on the other side of his desk. What the hell did he expect? She never knew where she was with him. He was as changeable as English weather.

'So? I'm not exactly overworked. And, that being the case, I think I'd better go and offer my services.'

He nodded. 'I suppose so. And I need to set the wheels in motion to find out if there's an underlying cause for Abe's anaemia.'

She drained her coffee-mug and moved to the door.

'Serina?'

'Yes?'

'You don't have to wait for Coral. I'll take you home.'

Within minutes she found herself serving the residents with tea and assisting those who needed help, but she found it exceedingly difficult to keep her mind on what she was doing.

Greg came in search of her just after seven. 'Finished here?'

Unsure if she could handle an evening at the farm with him when Coral and Heather weren't there, she murmured, 'I haven't seen Abe yet.'

'I've just left him. He's asleep.'

She followed him into his office. 'I don't mind waiting. Coral won't be long and you must be tired after your drive back from Jasper. It's a long way.'

'This isn't England.'

'Maybe, but Heather was saying that her journeys to and from work were more than enough driving for her.'

'That's not surprising.'

'Greg, while we're on the subject of Heather, I never thanked you properly for your help yesterday.'

'I did nothing. The problem resolved itself.'

'So I gather, but I'd love to know why you were so sure that sexually transmitted disease wasn't a problem. Did Danny convince you it was his first time. . .or. . .?' Her voice trailed off as she sought for an alternative.

Greg grinned wickedly. 'Something much more believable. I'll tell you because, as a fellow professional, I know I can trust you not to breathe a word to Heather or anyone else.'

Intrigued, Serina promised that she wouldn't.

'Danny, too, had been drinking that night. Rather more than was good for him.' His laugh was wicked.

'And?' she prompted.

'The inevitable—he couldn't, and Heather fell asleep and didn't know he hadn't. That's why Danny refused to discuss things with her the next day. Can you imagine a red-blooded youngster like him relishing telling her that he couldn't manage it?'

Serina joined in his laughter. 'Didn't Shakespeare say something very apt on that subject?'

'Yes. In Macbeth. I can't remember the exact words, but it was something about alcohol heightening the desire but weakening the ability.'

'Is that why you never drink?' she teased, realising the moment she had said it that she was treading dangerously.

'It could be because I'm always driving!'

Hearing reproach in his response, she retorted, 'I told you I'd wait for Coral.'

He took her hand between his and when their eyes met she could see laughter there. 'I didn't intend it as a criticism—I just thought I needed to defend my manhood!' He gave her a lopsided grin. 'Actually, I enjoy driving. So, as I'm off on Sunday, how about a trip to the Badlands?'

'The Badlands?'

'You remember, where they find so many dinosaur relics? I'd like to keep my promise to show them to you before you go home.'

'I'd like that, as long as Coral doesn't need me. I leave quite early on Monday so I must check.'

She saw a glint of amusement in his eyes. 'She doesn't. I'm ahead of you. I asked her permission when she arrived this evening.'

'What—?'

He laughed. 'You can enjoy the day away with a clear conscience.'

Aware that she'd been outmanoeuvred, she nodded.

He grinned. 'Great. We'll paint the town of Drumheller red. That'll give you something to remember me by.'

As if she would need anything!

He tried to describe what they would be seeing, but she found it difficult to visualise. 'You'll just have to wait and see,' he told her. 'I can guarantee you won't be disappointed.'

Coral knocked and came into the office at that moment.

'I'll drive you both home this evening,' Greg told them, and when they arrived at the farm it was as if his wishes were being answered. Coral didn't give them a moment alone. Eventually, with a rueful grin, he gave Serina a chaste goodnight kiss and they made their way to their respective beds.

CHAPTER ELEVEN

ONCE again, when Serina made her way up to the kitchen, Greg was up before her. If he was always such an early riser perhaps they weren't compatible at all!

'I hear you're visiting the Badlands on Sunday,' Coral told her, 'so I've been thinking. Greg and I are leaving soon as I'd like to see Ed. I wondered if you'd like to come in with me and we'll play truant this afternoon so that I can give you a whizz tour of the city. Otherwise you won't have a chance to see it.'

'What about Heather?'

Coral shrugged. 'She's disappeared to spend the day with Danny. His father collected her. I didn't know she knew this hour of the day existed!'

'How is he?'

'Doing well, by all accounts. He says he'll be back next Monday if the harvest isn't already finished. Somehow I think it will be. Scott is an extremely hard worker.'

'Will he be all right with nobody here all day?'

'I think so. We'll pop in at lunchtime, but I don't think it's really necessary. He's like Ed. Double-checks his every move, They'd get on well together.'

Patrick was at the reception desk when they arrived at the unit. When he saw Serina he said, 'You don't know how glad I am to see you. Abe keeps asking when you're coming in again.'

'Coral and I are going sightseeing this afternoon so I'll spend some time with him this morning. I've been writing up all he told me yesterday, and there's several bits I want to check out. He's OK, is he?'

'We considered a blood transfusion but, on balance, we think the distress it would cause would outweigh the benefit so we've started him on oral medication. Apart from that, no problem.'

After checking with Kathy that they weren't in desperate

164

need of her help, Serina went in search of Abe. She found
him, sitting alone in one of the comfortable day-rooms.
'Hi, how are you today?'

His face lit up when he saw her. 'All the better for a
sight of you,' he said, pulling an easy chair up closer.

The morning sped by as they chatted, and by the time
she walked down to the dining area with him Abe was as
animated as he had been the day before.

'I'm afraid this will probably be my last visit. I'm
returning to England on Monday.'

The elderly man's face fell. 'Can't you persuade her to
stay?' he asked Greg, who was walking along the corridor
towards them.

'If she wants to apply for permission to work over here
she has to do it from England. But I rather think that once
she gets back home you and I'll be forgotten.' As he spoke
his eyes held hers, dark and inscrutable.

Lowering her gaze, she muttered, 'I'll have Abe's life
story to remind me of him,' then added, for Greg's ears
only, 'but I'm not sure about you.'

Clearly taken aback, he patted Abe on the shoulder and
reassured him. 'I was only teasing. I'm sure she'll write.'

'I'm hoping to do something with all the information
you and others have given me,' she told Abe. 'When I
decide what I promise I'll send *you* the details.' She
stressed the 'you' for Greg's benefit, before steering Abe
to a seat in the dining-room.

Coral followed her in. 'Are you free to leave now?'

Serina nodded. 'Yep.'

'Let's go, then, before someone finds something suppos-
edly essential that they want done.'

When they reached the farm they found everything
going well as Coral had predicted so, after a quick snack,
they set out for the city. Serina enjoyed the afternoon,
fascinated by the way the relatively short history of the
area was preserved and presented for tourists.

The highlight of the afternoon was seeing the city
from the tallest tower. As Greg had told her, it was an incredible view and the weather was perfect. She could

have stayed there much longer, but she knew they had
to move on.

They were back in Greenfield in time for Coral to visit
Ed. Serina went with her. When they went into his room
he was chatting to Abe. He looked up with shining eyes
and told them, 'I can go home.'

'That's good,' Coral told him. 'I'll come and collect
you tomorrow.'

'I'm coming now. Greg says he can't get back to the
bungalow this evening so I'm coming instead.'

'I'll go and check—'

'You don't need to. I'm telling the truth.'

While Ed and Coral sorted out his belongings Serina
walked with Abe back to his room. As they reached the
door Ed called, 'I won't forget, Abe. Coral will bring
you out to see the farm one day next week, and we'll
talk more.'

Greg came along the corridor. 'Now Ed's going home,'
he told her, 'it won't matter if I stay at the hospital tonight
and give Patrick the day off tomorrow. Then I won't feel
so bad about leaving early on Sunday.'

It was late by the time they settled Ed, and Serina asked
Coral if she would be going into work the next day.

'I should, but I don't know if I can safely! I need to
keep an eye on him.'

'I'll do that and on Sunday as well, if you like. I don't
have to go to the Badlands if you're needed at the hospital.

'There's no need for that. Heather and Danny can spend
the day here instead of at his place. There'll be no
problem.'

Serina was doubtful. 'If you're sure, but I'll leave the
offer open. . .' She hesitated, before adding, 'Abe looked
really dejected when Ed said he was leaving.'

'We'll get him out here to chat with Ed, don't you
worry. I've done it before. It bucks them up no end.'

On Saturday morning Serina made a determined effort to
be up early and, taking the car, drove to Vegreville to pick

up some food for Coral and a few bits and pieces to take
home with her.

In one shop she found beautifully painted eggs that she
knew would remind her of the large Easter egg Greg had
taken her to see.

She arrived back at the farm in plenty of time to show
Coral her purchases before she had to leave for work.

After he'd had a rest Serina chatted to Ed for much of
the afternoon. He was able to fill in quite a lot of information about the early days that she'd missed in her notes.

'Those eggs you brought home today,' he told her, 'they
are made of decorated wood these days, but my dad blew
chicken eggs for Mom to decorate—she used different
plants for colouring.'

'Was that at Easter-time?'

He nodded. 'They symbolise resurrected life, you see.
The designs were different, according to where the family
originated. Dad gave Mom one when they were court-
ing—I believe I still have it somewhere. Most got smashed
over the years.'

'I'm glad you've told me all about them. They'll remind
me of your family when I'm back in England.' She sensed
that Ed was getting weary and suggested that she left
him to rest.

'I'll do that if you'll go out and check how that lad's
getting on.'

Serina did as he asked, but when she returned Ed was
asleep so she spent a quiet evening, mostly thinking about
her day out with Greg the next day and whether she would
ever see him again—or would her eggs be her only
reminder of him?

Despite being up even earlier on Sunday morning, Serina
found it difficult to decide what to wear for the trip to the
Badlands. If Greg still refused to be convinced that he had
a future she wanted to leave him with memories of her
that might just one day persuade him otherwise.

Unsure exactly what they'd be doing, rather than her
more usual jeans and T-shirt she donned a smarter pair
of trousers and a more formal blouse and jacket which,

nevertheless, were still comfortable for a day sightseeing.

'Will the journey take us long?' she asked as they made an early start from the bungalow.

'Two and a half to three hours.'

'Main roads, or dusty ones like this?'

'Mainly good roads and very, very, *very* straight.'

'What do you mean?'

Greg laughed. 'You wait and see.'

It wasn't long before Serina understood what he'd meant. She was already used to the flat prairie landscape but now they were travelling along, possibly, even flatter roads, and as there were no bends in sight she could see for miles both behind and ahead of them.

'It's incredible. However did they get the roads so straight?'

Greg turned to her with laughing eyes. 'Used a ruler.'

'A ruler? You're joking!'

'I mean it. When the settlers came to Alberta the land parcels were divided up on the map with ruled lines. Hence the roads in this part follow the lines.'

'We could do with roads like this in England.'

'Too true. I can't imagine you managing it, though. You've too much history that must be preserved.'

'At last! An admission that England has some good points.'

He turned and with a smile that sent a thrill of anticipation coursing through her veins said tenderly, 'You've changed my mind about the place. Any country that has produced you must have some good points.'

Aware that the colour was flooding into her cheeks, she murmured, 'You say that now you know I'm leaving.'

'You've been here more than long enough for me to know—without a doubt—that, if it were possible, you would be the only one for me.'

She sighed deeply. 'It is possible, Greg. I've told you again and again, but—'

He took a hand from the steering-wheel and, resting it lightly on her thigh, shook his head. 'Let's agree to differ, love, rather than spoil our last day together.'

Her heart plummeted as she recognised that his words

meant the end of her dreams, but at that moment an incredible vista opened up before them as the car began to descend into a canyon that until that moment had been hidden from view.

Forgetting her misery, Serina gasped at the sight of the sun-baked earth laid bare to reveal the secrets of the earth's formation over billions of years.

'It's unbelievable—like—like you imagine the moon's surface might be. It's so different to the prairie.'

'The valley was carved out by glaciers during the last ice age and, over the years since, the weather has continued the erosion.'

'There's not much vegetation, is there?'

'No. It's a patch of almost desert. Those flat-topped pillars you can see dotted around are formed by the wind and rain, scouring away the surrounding earth under the hard caps.'

There was so much to look at that Serina didn't speak again until they approached the town.

'We'll have a quick look at Drumheller itself and then go to the museum,' Greg told her.

As they drove into the town Serina saw references to dinosaurs everywhere and laughed. 'They certainly make the most of the tourist potential of the creatures, don't they?'

When Greg brought the car to a standstill she queried, 'Is this it? The centre?'

He laughed. 'Fraid so. Once a city serving a thriving coal mining area, it's tried to revive itself on the strength of the fossils to be found locally. I leave you to judge how successfully.'

'No comment, but let's try this museum I've heard so much about!'

They drove out of town again, and Serina asked him to stop so that she could take a closer look at the incredible landscape that surrounded them.

As she climbed from the car Greg joined her and they stood together, his arm encircling her shoulder.

'It's beautiful. Something I'll always remember. Thank you for bringing me.'

'Thank you for your company.' He bent and kissed her gently, but they were disturbed almost immediately by his mobile telephone, ringing inside the car.

'Who on earth can that be?'

It was Coral—with bad news. Serina was able to glean that much from his replies.

When he'd finished talking she asked, 'Is it Ed?'

He shook his head and said slowly, 'It's Gran. She's dead.' His flat statement seemed to make him take in for the first time that it was true, and he shuddered.

She wrapped her arms around him, 'Oh, Greg, I'm sorry. What happened?'

'She collapsed in the main street. Most likely a heart attack.' She felt him stir against her and then his lips touched her forehead. 'It's just come as such a shock.'

'At least she wouldn't have known much about it.' Already wondering how she would get back to the farm in time for her flight, she asked, 'Will you go straight to Jasper?'

He shook his head. 'As it's the weekend Brad's done what's necessary. I'll go on Monday after I've taken you to the airport. I can't sort anything out until then.'

He sighed heavily. 'I must ring my mother, though. I hadn't intended contacting her this weekend, but I'm afraid this news changes that.'

As he sat in the car and dialled his mother's number she wondered if he would normally have gone for a meal with her when he was in the area. If so, and he hadn't felt that he could acknowledge her presence to his mother, what hope did she have of ever becoming a part of his life?

Having completed his call, he leaned out of the car. 'Mum wanted to know what I was doing in the area, so I explained I was showing you the Badlands.'

She shook her head in disbelief. 'Does she know who I am?'

'Yes, and she wants me to take you for a meal this evening. Would you mind?'

'Not at all. Why should I? What did you say?'

'I accepted, but I can always ring back.'

'There's no need.'

'It won't be easy—' He took her hands between his. 'I didn't want to upset her more than necessary, but the last thing I want is for her to upset you.'

'Greg, I don't consider what happened in our parents' past has anything to do with me.'

'I know—that's what Mum's just been saying as well.'

Serina lifted a wry eyebrow. 'I'm glad to learn that at least one member of your family has some sense.'

'Are you saying I don't?' He assumed such a hurt expression that Serina had to choke back a laugh.

'I know you've plenty where your patients are concerned, but you don't apply it to your own situation.'

Watching a look of total denial register on his face, she knew that she wasn't getting through.

'Serina, I understand what you're trying to tell me, but I wish I could make you accept that I'm right. Gran's death endorses my decision.'

Serina looked at him with amazement. 'I don't believe it. You cast around for any excuse, don't you? Your grandmother certainly hasn't suffered her heart attack in the first flush of youth.'

She shook her head in disbelief. 'I'm beginning to wonder if you'll go to any length to avoid making a commitment. If I'm right, one thing I *am* grateful to you for is not giving in to my need for you to make love to me.'

He grasped both her arms firmly. 'Please, Serina, I know it can't be easy for you. It isn't for me, depite having lived with the decision for several years now. And, even though we don't know as yet what caused Gran's death, we *do* know she had Alzheimer's.'

'So?' Serina was becoming increasingly exasperated. 'Since when has that been hereditary? Although, come to think of it, perhaps the way you are behaving indicates that it could be setting in already.'

Her contempt made him grimace. 'Perhaps after you've met my mother you'll understand.'

Suddenly unwilling to continue what was clearly a losing battle, she urged, 'Come on. Let's make for the museum and not waste any more of my last day.'

They travelled only a short distance through more of

the unusual barren landscape before Greg swung the car into a side road to reveal a complex of roads, buildings and parking space that hadn't been immediately noticeable from the road.

As they walked across to the main entrance she was entranced by the excellent life-sized models of dinosaurs, flanking the front of the building, and from that moment she forgot her own problems and gave all her attention to the exhibits.

She soon found that the millions of years of history depicted within the museum put her concern about her own future into perspective. If Greg wasn't looking for anything more permanent than neither would she. She would enjoy the day out with him and then make a clean break and forget him. It wouldn't be easy but, after all, she had originally seen the trip to Canada as a break for freedom.

'There's so much,' she told him. 'I expected just dinosaur models, but I'm learning all the time. I know very little about the pre-history of the world. It's incredible—especially the plants—I never imagined someone working out a family tree for vegetation!'

He smiled indulgently and she could see that he was pleased she was enjoying it.

Over a snack lunch in the cafeteria she asked, 'Have you been here many times before?'

'Many, but I learn something new each time and, of course, some of the displays change regularly.'

After they'd eaten they spent another couple of hours wandering round the various galleries, Serina trying all the hands-on experiences available.

'It's after four,' he told her as they approached the exit. 'There are a couple more things I'd like to show you before we make our way home.'

The first was a tiny church—the smallest in the world—only big enough to seat six people. From there Greg drove a short distance and parked on the edge of a deep canyon. 'This is known as Horsethief Canyon.' He led her to the edge and slid an arm around her shoulders. 'It has a spectacular view of the valley.'

'It's mind-blowing. The way you can see the different layers that have formed over the ages. It's a geologist's dream.' She shook her head in wonderment. 'Horsethief Canyon—where did the name come from?'

'I believe the early settlers blamed the spirits of the canyon for the disappearance of their horses. In reality, I expect another group of settlers took them.'

When she had photographed and viewed the eroded slopes from every angle they returned to the car and drove past fields populated with small nodding pumps, extracting fuel from deep underground.

'What a strange sight,' Serina exclaimed. 'I thought at first they were animals.'

'They *are* known as nodding donkeys,' he grinned.

He stopped and slipped an arm along her shoulder as she photographed them. 'Mesmerising, aren't they?'

'I'll never forget this. It's like another world.'

As he hugged her to him he told her, 'It is. It's fantasy land, and when you are back home I hope that's how you'll remember our time together. As nothing more than a fantasy.'

'The holiday romance I didn't want,' she murmured.

'Romance, yes—affair, no. One day, when you're settled back in England, you'll be glad of that.'

'I'll let you know when that day arrives,' she told him flippantly, determined not to spoil their last day together.

Clearly relieved that she now accepted the situation, he told her, 'It'll be sooner than you think, I'm sure. Now, I'm afraid it's time to make tracks if we're not to be late for our meal. You're really sure you don't mind?'

'Of course not,' she told him as she climbed back into the car. 'I said so, didn't I?'

Despite her protestations, Serina was apprehensive as they drove to his mother's house. But she needn't have worried. Mrs Pardoe greeted her warmly, then held her at arm's length. 'She's just like her mother, Greg. Beautiful.'

He slipped a possessive arm round her shoulders. 'She is, isn't she?'

Unsure how he had portrayed her to his mother, Serina said, 'I'm only too grateful to Greg for giving up some of his time to show me your country.'

His mother looked surprised, but didn't comment. Instead, she took Serina's arm. 'Come through and find a seat until the food's ready. And do call me Sarah.'

Serina followed her along the short hall of the bungalow to a spacious lounge. While Sarah switched off the television she sat down on the edge of an enormous leather settee and looked around the comfortably furnished room.

Noticing her interest, Greg came and settled beside her. 'It's not a palace, but it has a very comfortable basement down below. Great for hibernation!'

Of course. She'd forgotten that it would have a lower floor.

'If the weather is bad they don't open the shop and Mother migrates downstairs. Come and see.'

As they went down the stairs Serina's gaze alighted on the library of books filling the opposite wall.

Greg showed her the two basement bedrooms with their own bathroom and she saw that one housed a gallery of photographs, most of them of Greg at different stages of his development. He was obviously his mother's pride and joy!

As they crossed to the shelves of books she murmured with a grin, 'I could adapt to this way of life very easily, I'd more than fill my time.'

He turned to her with eyebrows raised. 'Do you really think you would?'

Puzzled, and not a little affronted, she retorted, 'Of course. Wouldn't you expect me to?'

'You haven't been brought up to the life. I would have thought you'd have soon found it too isolated.'

Sarah called them at that moment so the conversation ended there, but it left Serina unhappy to learn that was still his impression of her.

The meal they shared was hearty and well cooked, something Serina had noticed applied to all the food she'd enjoyed since her arrival in Alberta.

Greg and his mother talked about the arrangements for his visit to Jasper the next day, and then turned the conversation to Serina and the voluntary work she was doing at Greenfield.

As the evening progressed she became uncomfortable at some of Sarah's extravagantly complimentary remarks. It seemed to Serina that she was trying to make amends for something she knew nothing about.

At least it was a relief to find that Greg's mother wasn't the ogre Serina had been expecting. Apart from the compliments, the evening had been enjoyable. Surely if her mother had done something awful Mrs Pardoe wouldn't make her feel quite so welcome?

When they were ready to leave Greg went to the bathroom and Sarah surprised her with a kiss on the cheek, before saying quietly, 'I wish I'd got in touch with your mother long ago, but I was too ashamed.'

It was clear that Sarah believed that Serina knew all about the events of the past, and she tried to say that she didn't.

Greg's mother wasn't listening. 'It was only drink that made me do it. We were such close friends until that night.'

Serina touched her arm lightly. 'Whatever it was, I'm sure Mum must have forgotten all about it. Otherwise she'd have said something to me, and she didn't. We had a happy life together and that's what I want to remember.' She took hold of Sarah's hand as Greg came towards them, and smiled. 'It's been a lovely evening.'

'You are so like your mother, in nature as well as looks. I look forward to meeting up with you again when you're next over here.'

'If I *do* come again I'd like that, but I've no plans to do so at the moment.'

Mrs Pardoe looked puzzled and, turning to Greg, told him sharply, 'We need to talk. I'll see you Monday in Jasper.'

He frowned. 'I should be there around lunchtime, provided Serina's plane leaves on time, but you don't have to come. I can deal with everything.'

'I want to.'

The moment his car was on the road he rested his hand on Serina's knee. 'Thank you.'

'What for?'

'Being there. I think you've gone some way to erasing Mum's bitter memories.'

'If I have I'm pleased.' Serina was quietly trying to make some sense of what his mother had said when Greg started to talk about his grandmother.

'You know, it was as if we made up for all the bad feeling last Wednesday when I went down to see her. I do wish Mum could have been there that day. Gran was quite lucid.'

'Mmm,' Serina answered absent-mindedly, before a sudden thought made her say excitedly, 'Greg! You don't think—?'

'Think what?'

'I wonder if she was lucid the day I saw her. You see, she said something like, ''It was not being his son that killed him''.'

'It doesn't really sound like sense to me.'

'I don't know. If she was talking about her son, your father—Greg, your mother has just told me something that makes me wonder. . .' She hesitated.

'Go on.'

Serina found it difficult. 'No. It's ridiculous. I'm just trying to plot a happy ending.'

He frowned. 'What on earth are you talking about?'

Serina couldn't hide the excitement bubbling inside her. 'Do you look like your father?'

'I haven't a clue. I told you I don't remember him.'

'There must have been photographs.'

Greg shrugged. 'I don't think so. Why?'

'I'm just wondering if. . .' She hesitated again, unsure how he might take her suggestion. 'Well, if perhaps your mother's husband wasn't your real father.'

His face furious, Greg pulled the car into the side of the road. 'That's a pretty vile accusation.'

'I don't mean it to be, Greg, but it was something your mother said when you went to the loo.'

'Yes?' he prompted.

'She apologised for whatever happened in the past and said, ''It was only drink that made me do it.'' She seemed to think I knew all about the quarrel, but I told her I didn't and didn't want to know. But now, remembering Heather saying the same thing the other day, perhaps I do.'

'I really don't know what you're trying to say,' Greg told her angrily, 'but I can put an end to it now because I know he was my father. His name is on my birth certificate.'

'Yes, but—'

'I don't want to hear any more. Mum would have told me long ago if that was the case. I'm damned if I'm going to allow you to say such things about her, especially when she can't defend herself.'

'But—' Serina took one look at Greg's set features and knew that it was hopeless.

She had been tactfully trying to work out how to suggest that as registrars weren't there at the conception the birth certificate might just be wrong. However, it was clear that he was too angry to even consider what she now believed was a distinct possibility.

As Greg restarted the engine she said, 'I liked your mother very much, and I'm sorry if you think I insulted her. I can assure you I won't mention it ever again.'

She shrank unhappily back on the passenger seat, her mind working overtime. Was she missing something? Had he known the truth all along and hadn't wanted to abandon the perfect excuse for making no commitment?

Was that why his behaviour had been so ambiguous? Had he, despite his protests, hoped she'd succumb and agree to an affair? If so, there was no point in trying to prove that she was right about his father.

She tried to blink back the tears that had been threatening, and resolved to make a clean break the moment they arrived in Greenfield. The last thing she wanted was a protracted leave-taking at the airport with someone she could no longer trust, even if she was still physically attracted to him.

Greg put the car into cruise control and surreptitiously stole a glance at Serina. Seeing her wet lashes, he berated himself for his violent reaction to her suggestion. He should have realised that she was only doing it because she loved him and wanted to find some explanation, however fanciful, that would persuade him that they had a future together.

The trouble was that, throughout his life, he'd always had to be there for his mother because there'd never been anyone else, but suddenly it had turned sour on him. He'd automatically struck out in defence of her reputation rather than believe that the one girl he had ever loved might just be right.

Was it remotely possible? Stranger things had happened. Oh, why hadn't he listened instead of losing his temper? He knew it was a faint chance but he needed to check— and certainly before he raised her hopes again. He'd hurt her far too much already.

In the meantime, though, he must apologise. As they approached Greenfield he rested a hand on her thigh and murmured, 'I'm sorry. I—I—'

She shrank further away from him. 'There's nothing to be sorry for, Greg. I've had a super time but I think, for both our sakes, the sooner we make the break the better. I hate protracted farewells so I'm sure Coral will drop me at the airport on her way to work.'

CHAPTER TWELVE

TURNING his head to look at her, Greg smiled ruefully. 'I understand why you said what you did, Serina, but I shouldn't have reacted that way. It's just that, over the years, I've automatically stood up for my mother, whatever the crisis. And there have been plenty.'

He took hold of her nearest hand. 'I certainly didn't mean to upset you. I think far too much of you for that.'

No longer prepared to boost his ego, she said brightly, as if she hadn't heard a word he'd said, 'If we're back in time I'd like to pop into the unit and say goodbye to everyone, especially Abe.'

He sighed. 'I think we can arrange that.'

It was dark when he pulled into the car park and she slid from the car before he could unfasten his seat belt. 'I'm going to see Abe.'

She passed Coral in the corridor. 'Hi. How's it going?'

'Fine. Have you had a good day?'

Serina nodded.

'Sorry I had to ring with the bad news.'

Serina smiled to reassure her. 'It was a good thing, actually. It meant I met up with Mrs Pardoe, which I wouldn't have done otherwise.'

Coral's eyes widened with horror. 'Was she. . .?'

'She was fine. She didn't appear to bear a grudge against me so we had a pleasant evening. It must have become blown out of all proportion and I hope that's the end of it. Anyway, how's Ed?'

'Not bad at all. Danny and Heather are at the farm with him.'

'When will you finish here?'

'Eleven, as usual.'

'In that case, I think I'll come back to the farm

179

with you, then. And I wonder if you'd be able to run me to the airport on your way to work tomorrow?'

Although obviously surprised that Greg wasn't taking her, she asked no questions. 'No problem. Heather will be home. Danny is hoping to start combining again in the morning.'

'Thanks, Coral.'

Having said her goodbyes to Abe and the staff she had now come to know so well, she made her way to Greg's office and found him closeted with Patrick.

'Come in, Serina,' Patrick invited. 'I'm off in a moment. We were just discussing Mrs Loziac. You remember her? On the acute wing?'

Serina nodded. 'You were waiting to see the outcome of the chemotherapy.'

'That's right. She's been home for the weekend and has coped so well that her husband and family want her to stay there for the time being. She'll be delighted. It should do her a lot of good.'

'What happened to the chap with the fractured hip who was transferred the same day?'

'He did incredibly well and was discharged last week. So it's been a peaceful weekend. You should take more time off, Greg!' He turned and, about to shake Serina's hand, pulled her towards him instead. 'Aw, I think I know you well enough by this time to give you a goodbye kiss.'

'Ready to leave?' Greg asked her as Patrick disappeared through the door.

'I've arranged to go back with Coral. It'll save you a journey.'

'But—' She could see that he was hurt, but refused to allow that to influence her.

'I'll take you to the airport tomorrow.'

'No need, Coral's taking me.'

He was silent for a long moment, before saying quietly, 'I'd like to take you.'

Although her heart ached at the thought of never seeing him again she knew that every moment more spent together would make it worse, so she told him firmly, 'I think it's better this way, Greg. As I said, I don't like long goodbyes. And you have to make your way to Jasper.'

If she hadn't hurt so much inside herself the expression of disbelief on his face would have amused her.

'I'll have plenty of time to go there after I've seen you off. There's no hurry.'

She shook her head. 'Maybe not, but I've made my decision and I'd rather make it a clean break.'

He swept her up into his arms and kissed her deeply. before moaning softly, 'I'm sorry, love. Really, really sorry it had to end this way.'

When Coral came in search of her they were locked silently in each other's arms.

Serina resolutely pulled herself free. 'Goodbye, Greg. And thank you for everything.'

On the way home Coral could curb her curiosity no longer. 'I was sure Greg would take you to the airport. Can't Patrick stand in for him?'

Serina shook her head. 'Greg has to go to Jasper.'

'Will you be coming back to Alberta soon?'

'I don't think so, Coral. I've loved my time with you, but I think it's time for me to find myself a proper job again and settle down.'

'In England?'

'Probably. Hopefully there'll be more nursing jobs going over there than there are here at the moment.'

'But what about Greg?'

'What about him?' Serina replied quietly as Coral pulled up outside the bungalow. 'I've enjoyed the time I've spent with him, but that's all there is to it. There's no future for us.'

Heather and Ed were both asleep so Serina made the two of them a cup of coffee. When they were settled in the lounge Coral put her earlier question even more bluntly.

'Will Greg be visiting you in England?'

'I shouldn't think so for one moment.'

'But why? I was so. . .' She paused, unsure if she should go on.

Her obvious concern brought forth the flood of tears Serina had bottled up all weekend.

Rushing to her side, Coral murmured, 'I'm so sorry, love. Was it his mother?'

When Serina didn't answer she continued, 'She's been so bitter for so long that I can see her taking pleasure in ruining everyone else's happiness.'

Swallowing hard, Serina shook her head. 'It's not his mother. She was great. It's Greg,' she sobbed.

Coral frowned. 'Greg? I don't understand.'

'It's all tied up with his childhood. He says he's so afraid he'll die young like his father and grandfather did that he won't consider marrying. In case he leaves his wife to cope alone.'

Coral frowned. 'I see, but—'

'Long before he met me he'd made up his mind not to marry and nothing, not even love, seems able to change his mind. In a way I began to admire him, seeing him as the original Mr Nice Guy who's prepared to forfeit his own happiness to spare anyone else pain, but today I realised that he could be using it to avoid a commitment and it hurts.'

Coral held her close until her misery began to subside. 'You poor love. And there's me thinking how well suited you were to one another and pushing you together.'

Serina gave her a watery smile. 'It was all over an hour ago. We've agreed a clean break is best so please forget I've told you any of this and, especially, don't say anything to Greg.'

On her arrival at the airport Serina first needed to check that her flight was on schedule.

Whilst she waited in line her thoughts wandered over all that had happened since the day she'd arrived there.

Although the ache in her heart wasn't any easier at least the uncertainty she'd lived with during her time in Alberta was over. She now knew for sure that she would never see Greg Pardoe again.

Despite her desperate attempts to persuade him that even one year's happiness would more than make up for any number of future years alone, he hadn't wanted to hear.

So, a complete break had been the only answer.

She made her way back to Coral, who was watching her luggage trolley. 'I can book in soon. Would you like a coffee before I disappear?'

Coral shook her head. 'No, thanks. I must make a move, if you're sure you'll be OK on your own.'

Serina grinned. 'No problem. I got here on my own, didn't I?' Serina kissed her warmly. 'Thanks for everything, Coral. I've really had a smashing time.'

'We've loved having you. Please come again, but for a proper holiday next time.'

'It's your turn to visit me. Don't forget. Heather wants to see London.' Noting that Coral's eyes were suspiciously bright, she smiled and—lifting her cases—said, 'Thanks again, it's been great,' and strode off to the check-in desk before tears could gather in her own eyes.

As the queue moved slowly forward the thought of all the friends she'd made in such a short time made the prospect of her arrival in England, with no one to meet her, even more bleak.

When the clerk beckoned her forward she bent her knees to pick up her cases, only to find the large one whisked away from her grasp.

She started to yell a protest but then saw Greg, clutching his briefcase in one hand, lifting her case onto the scale.

'What—?' she gasped. At the same moment the clerk demanded, 'Ticket? Passport?'

She tried to concentrate on what she was doing, but her thoughts refused to co-operate. She was angry that he'd come, despite her asking him not to, and she dropped one thing after another from her handbag.

Greg retrieved all her bits and pieces and then her hand luggage.

'Would you please give me back my property,'

she demanded as she moved away from the booking-in desk.

He ignored her request and placed her hand luggage with his briefcase on a trolley.

As she attempted to retrieve her bag she wondered incongruously if he never went anywhere without his briefcase.

Gently removing her hand from her bag, he pulled her towards him and into his arms.

'Greg,' she admonished angrily. 'I told you not to come—'

He silenced her protest with a kiss. When he eventually released her he murmured, 'I couldn't let you walk out of my life like this.'

Resisting his embrace, she murmured, 'You couldn't?' Surely her decision to make a clean break hadn't achieved what all her reasoning had failed to do?

'Come over here and sit down.'

She did as he said, and waited suspiciously for his next words.

His eyes held hers with an impassioned plea, and his emotions appeared so strong that he had to swallow repeatedly before he could speak.

'Knowing that I wouldn't see you again spurred me into action because the moment you walked out of my office door I knew that I didn't want to live without you. But I wanted to be fair to you as well, love.'

So, what was he trying to tell her? That he'd moved a small way but not done a complete U-turn? Was he still hoping for an affair? If so, he was too darned late.

'I'm sorry I was so angry yesterday when you tried to tell me about my father.'

She shrugged. 'I should have realised how upset you would be. You're as close to your mother as I was to mine. I guess that's one of the drawbacks of having a single parent. I'm sorry I said what I did Greg, but—'

'I'm glad you did.' Regardless of the many onlookers, her kissed her again and again. 'You see,' he told her jubilantly, 'I started to think about the situation when you left, and overnight lots of things that have been said in the past began to add up.

'So I rang my mother at first light, demanding to know the truth.' He kissed her with a frantic urgency.

'You were right, love, so right. I don't look at all like her husband because he wasn't my father. That's why there were no photographs. Mum destroyed them all so I'd never know. Apparently Gran was furious about that.'

Serina gasped. 'But your mother—'

He laughed ruefully. 'After all these years of harbouring bitterness, she said that the moment she saw you she realised what a fool she'd been—that your mother had known what she was doing when she broke off her engagement. If her fiancé had really loved her he wouldn't have been tempted by Mum or anyone else.

'She liked you, Serina. Almost as much I love you.' His lips met hers with a gentle certainty and she relaxed in his arms, although she couldn't help thinking that all this had come too late.

'So what—' Her words were drowned by a voice on the loudspeaker, announcing that her plane was loading.

She flung him a stricken look and lifted her bag from the trolley. 'I'm sorry, Greg. I have to go.'

'So do I.'

Of course, he had to go to Jasper. 'I'll say goodbye, then—'

He laughed and lifted his briefcase from the trolley. 'Goodbye? I'm coming with you!'

'You're what?'

'I booked my seat next to yours long before you arrived.'

'I can't believe it. . .'

She still didn't move but frowned suddenly. 'But what are you doing, coming to England? What about the unit? Your patients? *And* your trip to Jasper?'

He slung his free arm around her shoulder and, urging her towards the departure lounge, teased, 'You worry too much. Patrick's a good friend. He's going to hold the fort for a couple of days. And Mum's going to Jasper to make all the arrangements and I can be back in time for the funeral.'

'But your mother—'

'She wants to make amends, not only for keeping the truth from me but for not being able to cope with Gran when she was alive. It'll be good therapy for her.

'You see, even if you hadn't sussed out the truth she would have told me now that Gran's dead. That was why she wanted to see me in Jasper so urgently. I think she must have guessed I was holding out on marriage when you told her that you probably wouldn't be back in Canada.'

'Me and my big mouth again.'

'I know a good way to deal with that,' he laughed, kissing her repeatedly as they shuffled forward.

He had to release her as they clambered onto the plane, but the moment they were seated she snuggled against him and said, 'I still can't believe this. But I wish it was for more than two days.'

'Hopefully it'll be long enough to set the wheels in motion for your migration to Canada. Especially as we have a secret weapon to speed the process.'

'What's that?' she asked as he took the seat beside her.

'Marriage. You will say yes, won't you? I'm banking on it.'

She giggled. 'Only if you come with a guarantee!'

'I thought you were prepared to take a risk.' He swept her into his arms and his lips pressed firmly against hers, as if attempting to prove—with or without a guarantee— that he was worth consideration.

Her breath quickened as her lips parted, allowing him to deepen his kiss until such a helpless, drowning sensation overwhelmed her that she knew there could never be anyone else.

When he eventually released her from his arms so that she could fasten her seat belt she asked tentatively, 'Do you know who your father is?'

'His name, yes, and the fact that he was a surgeon. But I don't intend to look him up. I think the past needs to be buried once and for all before anyone else gets hurt.

'When I first met you I was so fired up on Mum's behalf. I knew someone Mum had trained with was the cause of her bitterness, and it seemed to me that if your mother hadn't mentioned her then she must be the one. And I suppose it was because I was so attracted to you that I was pulled in two directions. Otherwise, I would never have allowed myself to imagine all manner of dreadful things about you. As you know, I even wondered if you might be sponging on Coral!'

'I remember. I was furious that day at the unit. . .'

He leaned over and kissed her. 'By the time I told you that, I knew better. That you are the most beautiful, loving, caring, clever, efficient, professional, adaptable person I've ever known. In fact, you're just perfect.'

She snuggled her head onto his shoulder. 'I kept hoping you might realise it.'

'One thing is worrying me, though. Winter's approaching fast and by the time you get everything organised your end the temperatures here could be minus forty. Do you think you'll cope?'

'Perhaps we could move into a house with a cosy basement and hibernate down there together.'

'Someone will have to earn us a living!'

'I know, but we could have a honeymoon there. And I could use all the information I've been collecting to write a best-seller. Then you wouldn't have to work!'

He laughed and hugged her to him. 'I think it'll take more than a history of Alberta to do that.'

He released her sufficiently to be able to kiss her again. 'As I've said before, you're awesome. So often in the past couple of weeks you've commented on how much you enjoy our more relaxed way of life, but I'm still worried that you might miss the high life you're used to back home.'

'As *I've* said before, you're a fool, Greg Pardoe. We don't all live in London. I come from a rural backwater and hate city life as much as you do.'

'I love you, Serina Grant.'

'And I love you, Greg, as I believe I've told you before.'

He grinned wickedly. 'But this time I'm in a position

to do something about it. I can't wait until I get you off this plane.'

As the plane climbed rapidly from the runway he watched the rosy tint touching her cheek and whispered, 'Unless you'd like to join the mile-high club?'

She pretended to be scandalised and then laughed. 'I don't think so. You see, I don't believe in holiday romances. I'll wait until we're back on English soil.'

DISCOVER

THE SECRETS WITHIN

*Riveting and unforgettable -
the Australian saga of the decade!*

*For Tamara Vandelier, the final reckoning with
her mother is long overdue. Now she has
returned to the family's vineyard estate and
embarked on a destructive course that, in a
final, fatal clash, will reveal the secrets within....*

Valid only in the UK & Eire against purchases made in retail outlets
and not in conjunction with any Reader Service or other offer.

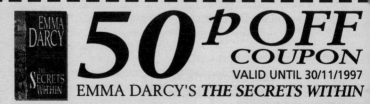

50p OFF COUPON

VALID UNTIL 30/11/1997

EMMA DARCY'S *THE SECRETS WITHIN*

To the Customer: This coupon can be used in part payment for
a copy of Emma Darcy's THE SECRETS WITHIN. Only one coupon
can be used against each copy purchased. Valid only in the UK
& Eire against purchases made in retail outlets and not in
conjunction with any Reader Service or other offer. Please do
not attempt to redeem this coupon against any other product
as refusal to accept may cause embarrassment and delay at the
checkout.
To the Retailer: Harlequin Mills & Boon will redeem this coupon
at face value provided only that it has been taken in part
payment for a copy of Emma Darcy's THE SECRETS WITHIN.
The company reserves the right to refuse payment against
misredeemed coupons. Please submit coupons to: Harlequin
Mills & Boon Ltd. NCH Dept 730, Corby, Northants NN17 1NN.

9 904170 180504

0472 00166